Stories to a Restless Billionaire

SUKHVINDER SINGH

INDIA • SINGAPORE • MALAYSIA

ISBN 979-8-88986-937-5

DISCLAIMER

The information provided within this Book is for general informational purposes only. While we try to keep the information up-to-date and correct, there are no representations or warranties, express or implied, about the completeness, accuracy, reliability, suitability or availability with respect to the information, products, services, or related graphics contained in this Book for any purpose. Any use of the methods describe within this Book are the author's personal thoughts. They are not intended to be a definitive set of instructions for this project. You may discover there are other methods and materials to accomplish the same end result.

Names and persons in this book are entirely fictional. They bear no resemblance to anyone living or dead.

CONTENTS

ACKNOWLEDGEMENT

I would like to thank my wife, for all her support and encouragement. I am also thankful to my entire family, which includes my parents and my brother for their unconditional love and support. It is through the teaching of my parents and their upbringing, that I could assimilate all the wisdom and write this book.

INTRODUCTION

Once there was man named William Bill. He was quite ambitious, zealous and a man of strong Intellect. He wanted to become the richest man of the world. He was very passionate about his work. Bill's parents were rich, and he was raised in affluence. As Bill completed his graduation, he took over his father's business and employed Steve, his best friend as the CEO in his company.

Steve and Bill were childhood friends. They lived in the same village, studied in the same school, and had an irrevocable bonding. Steve belonged to a typical middle-class family. Steve grew up in a home steeped in truth, ethics, and compassion. Steve's father was a learned man and worked as a school teacher, whereas his mother was totally absorbed in religion. She devoted all her time to the family, church and helping the poor and the needy.

Steve was thoughtful, gallant, and purposeful. Bill and Steve had a good bonding, trust and understanding. This association turned fruitful for both. As days passed Bill started becoming wealthier.

One day Bill called Steve and said, "Steve, I want you to go all around the country and study how people are making money. Study the economic affairs, various markets and commodities, study the latest tricks of the trade, identify emerging markets producing stellar returns and tell me how to become the richest man in this country.

Further Steve, I am also keen to know what people are doing. So, study people of different cultures, different caste, different age groups, different status, educated and the uneducated, poor and the rich, good and the bad and so on. I want you to collect all the data with respect to their activities."

Steve was quite surprised, as this was a very painstaking job.

He replied, "Bill this is an onerous task, which requires a lot of hard work, perseverance and dedicated efforts."

Bill replied, "Don't worry Steve, you will not go alone, you will be accompanied by several other wise people, who will assist you in this assignment. You will receive the best of facilities, under my auspices. However, I want you to take this task immediately and execute it with all your heart and soul."

Having no choice, Steve acquiesced Bill's decision and accepted the formidable task. Steve travelled all around the country, studied all different kind of businesses, the economic affairs and people of various cultures, religions, different societies, etc. On acquiring the data, Steve would regularly send it to Bill. Bill started becoming richer, day by day. Steve completed the grueling task conscientiously and returned back. Within few years, Bill amassed immense wealth and became the richest man in the whole of America.

One day Bill again called Steve and said, "I have become the richest man of U.S. and now I want to become the richest man of the world. So, I want you to go all around the world and study the business affairs, various markets and commodities and share with me, all those prospective opportunities, which can make me the wealthiest man on earth. Also study people all around the world and let me know, the major activities people are involved in."

Steve being aware that Bill has become more capricious and erratic in his management style, hence it was futile to argue with him. Despite feeling totally exasperated, Steve set out on this circuitous journey. Steve starts collecting all the data of the world and sends it to Bill. Bill is now becoming richer than ever. In a few years' time, Bill becomes the richest man of the world and is now at the zenith of his achievements. Steve now returns back.

By this time Bill is almost 45 years old. Bill seems to be more tensed now. Stress is clearly visible on his face. Bill is becoming more fastidious and very irascible.

Once again Bill calls Steve and says, "Steve, I want you to share all the data of what people are doing in this world. I am the richest, but now I want to have all the power and authority. I want to have my control over everything. I want to become the most powerful and influential person on earth. Hence, I want all the data."

Steve replies, "Bill I have already shared all the data with you. It is with you."

Bill replies in a supercilious tone, "I know Steve. I want you to squeeze and filter all the data scrupulously and share the one which is most important."

Once again Bill assigns assiduous task to Steve, which requires a lot of hard work and patience. However, Steve agrees, albeit reluctantly.

After working for few years, Steve returns with one hundred files. On seeing the files, Bill becomes incredibly happy.

He starts reading the files and all its contents. Time goes by. However, it is not easy for Bill to read these hundred files, which is full of convoluted information. His eyesight is now weak, he has floaters in his eyes. He also has migraine. All the tensions and anxieties of business are multiplying the infirmities of age. Moreover, Bill is ignoring his health, blithely.

Bill once again calls Steve and says, "Steve, I want you to work on all this data. I am the wealthiest man of this world and I want to become the most powerful man on earth. I want everything to be under my influence and my control."

Steve realizes that Bill is plagued by avarice and a thirst for power; hence curtailing his sensibility and making him insane. He seems to have lost his poise, his ability to think clearly. Bill is losing his mental balance.

Steve, who could no longer take this interminable and lousy task, loses his patience, and leaves the room, with disdain. He could not attune himself to Bill's importunate expectations. Next day Steve sends his resignation letter and leaves Bill forever.

Bill becomes very upset. It is pathetic to lose Steve. Bill realizes that he has been behaving quite irrationally with Steve. He also realizes that he is like the old lion who has reached the end of his tether. It's a great loss.

After a few years, Bill becomes very ill. A team of the best doctors come to examine, only to find that Bill has a malignant tumor in his brain, which can neither be operated nor be cured, by any means. This was an insidious onset of an incurable disease.

As per the prognosis the doctors inform, "Bill you have hardly few months or maximum of one year to live. Just do what is most important in your life. There is nothing more we can do medically."

It was a shocking news, which came unheralded. Bill was baffled. He could not sleep whole night. He was totally exasperated. Life came in total dismay and despondency. There was complete darkness. All his riches, power, luxuries, assets, authority, all the data of the world, through which he wanted to become the most powerful person in the world, seemed to be worthless. Everything seemed to be futile now.

Bill became more confused than ever, as life was in utter desolation. Bill who always had the habit of commanding all the situations, felt totally helpless, when his own life was completely beyond his control. Bill, inspite of all his power and wealth, was totally constrained to avert the uncertainties of life. His business was faltering and life ebbing away. He felt as if he had missed the bus – the most important essence of life. Life seemed to have just passed away within a blink of an eye. Everything seemed like a dream – a bad dream with a terrible ending. He felt as if he has been cheated by his own life. The situation was incomprehensible. Bill was now plodding away day and night, confused and totally wretched.

Bill wondered what the purpose of life is. Bill wondered!!

Who am I?
Why this happened to me?
Was I supposed to take birth and just die?
What is the purpose of human life and this creation?
Who is God?
Why am I here?
What happens after death?
What is the ultimate destiny of every human being?
What is enlightenment?

Hundreds of questions popped up into Bill's mind with no answers, creating more anxiety.

There was an intense desire to know life which has slipped out of his hands, so meaninglessly. Bill was inundated with unanswerable questions. He was lost in the labyrinth of his disturbing thoughts, inexplicable questions and became totally restless.

He lost interest in everything that he used to enjoy the most in his life. He loved playing golf, visiting good places, enjoying his morning coffee, reading newspaper, listening to music, solitary drinking, driving his luxurious sports cars, socializing with his friends, lavish fetes, talking to his secretary sometimes and sharing about his achievements, etc. Now suddenly all these things had no meaning. All, for which he was so passionate, became purposeless. Life seemed to have lost all its savor. Bill was deprived of all the enthusiasm in his life, in utter lassitude. He could not sleep well. Mornings were more tiring than evenings, since he could see the sunset of his life, at every moment. Days were pitch black. Bill now sat brooding over his fate and worrying about his future, totally addled. Time was running pretty hard.

With all the confusion going in Bill's mind, Bill recalled Steve, who could be his stalwart in such trying times. The only man he trusted, who was wise, candor and who could probably enlighten him. The man with whom Bill could wear his heart on his sleeve, who could answer all his questions and could confide in.

So, the next morning Bill asked one of his managers to search for Steve and tell him that Bill has requested to meet him as soon as possible.

In this modern world of technology and communication with mobiles and emails, Steve was easily located and the message entreating him to see Bill, reached quickly.

Though Steve never intended to see Bill, but the information that Bill was gravely ill and wanted to see him as early as possible, made Steve realize the seriousness of the situation and he assented to see Bill.

A special helicopter was sent to receive Steve. Steve is now back.

On seeing Bill, Steve is surprised, as Bill's body has become more corpulent, his face has turned pale with sunken eyes and surfeited with depression. Bill was totally incapacitated by his illness.

However, Bill, on seeing Steve, feels very happy, as if a gleam of hope has emerged in his dark life.

Bill greets Steve with respect. However, Bill still has that arrogance, that feeling of condescension and he still expects Steve to behave like his employee, to be under his command.

Bill asks Steve impatiently in a peremptory tone, "Steve, I want you to share with me all the wisdom of this life. I have a lot of questions about life. I can pay you whatever you want. I want you to live here with me and answer all my questions."

Steve who is no more the employee of Bill, smelling that arrogance of Bill, replies with temerity, "Bill, I understand your situation. But unfortunately, I am busy, and I don't have the time to share all the wisdom with a man who has lost his war. A man, whose mind seems like a barren land, where I don't expect the seeds of any merits to grow. I don't want to waste my efforts anymore. Keep your money with you Bill."

Bill did not expect such a blunt reply, feels angry and replies impudently, "Steve, today when I am losing my balls, you have gathered the strength to speak, but there was a time when people used to wag their tails like dogs in front of me."

"People used to wag their tails like dogs because they did not want the bigger dog to bark," Steve retorted.

Bill feels very agitated on Steve's answer. He pounds his fist on the table and angrily shouts, "Do you mean to say that I am a dog?"

Bill wants to shout more and retort, but he has a wheezy chest and is convulsed with a hacking cough like a ninety-year-old man.

On seeing Bill's condition, Steve commiserates, "Bill, calm down. I don't mean to say that you are a dog. Don't get me wrong, but there was a dog within you, who would go out of control sometimes."

Bill who is internally weak and frail, whose illness has debilitated him completely, realizes that he is out of options. He understands that his arrogance and arguments would exacerbate the situation and he cannot afford to lose Steve this time. Hence, he pauses for a moment, thinks wisely and replies in a tremulous tone, "You are right Steve, we all have these animals within us. We are born as human beings, but we have the capability to become divine and animal both. Probably in greed of making more money and in my selfish interests, I don't know which animal I fostered more within me. I always thought it was a lion but perhaps you are right it may have been a dog. I think I am paying the price now."

Bill in a contrite tone continues, "Steve I am sorry, I know I was very irrational with you, I was selfish and sometimes imbecile. I apologize for my arrogance and condescending behavior. However, I have learned my lessons. Probably you don't know about my health. I have only few months to live. I don't know whether I will be able to see the next Christmas or not. I am confused, stressed, and completely depressed in my life. I am tired. I am mentally exhausted. Everything is finished in my life."

Bill looking beseechingly at Steve, now requests, "I wanted to see you, not only because you were my best friend, but since you have always been a man of poise and clarity. I always admired your skills. Your wisdom and eloquence are laudable. You know me very well, you know my weaknesses, you know my flaws, you know my strengths. I want you to share with me the wisdom you think is appropriate. It would be an honor if you could enlighten my soul before it becomes a victim of my sick mind. You are my last resort, Steve."

Steve's heart fills with compassion as he realizes that he cannot forsake Bill at this stage; after all they have been buddies for years and it's time when Bill needs him the most.

Steve says, "OK Bill. I was aware one day you would call me, considering the vagaries of life you were leading. It is not surprising that I am standing in front of you once again. However, looking to your last desire, I would share all the wisdom with you. I would sit with you every day and share all that is important in life, I would reveal all the wisdom into stories. I know Bill, you are fond of stories. When we were small, you wanted my company just to listen to stories from me.

I assure, that you will atleast not go bare handed from this world. Apart from the balance sheet of your assets and money, which are now totally worthless, you will have something that will enrich your heart and soul."

Listening to this Bill feels quite relived and exulted. He thanks Steve for his generosity.

Dear readers, the chapters of this book have various stories and parables which Steve shares with Bill, who is one of the wealthiest men of the world, but also the most restless now. Every story is reinforced with wisdom, the purpose of this creation and eventually understanding life with a different perspective. Since Bill is not an easy person, he is not going to get convinced with any fairy tale. Hence sometimes Steve is confronted with various questions during his conversation. However, Steve replies to all his questions very candidly and concisely. This interesting conversation between Bill and Steve enlightens us and provides more clarity towards the fundamental aspects of life, especially today's life, where we are in the mad rush of digital world, a world of Artificial Intelligence, compelling us to move at its own speed and orientation, and sometimes making us also restless, like Bill.

Like in mathematics it is said that the shortest distance between two points is a straight line. Similarly, the shortest way between a human intellect and truth is a small story. I am sharing all the important knowledge and wisdom in the form of stories. I hope my readers would be greatly benefitted from the contents of this book.

Chapter 1

ONE THING WITH WHICH WE PLAY EVERY MOMENT AND THROUGHOUT OUR LIFE

It is the first day of the session when Steve comes to meet Bill. Bill now walks with a stick in his hand, his voice has become soft. After the heated conversation, Bill's arrogance seems to be fading away and Bill is becoming quite humble. However, Bill seems to be quite enervated and confused with his life.

He has an opulent mansion. The place is very lavish. Rooms are uncountable. Every nook and corner in the house, is a piece of art. The interiors are sumptuous with intricate design. Everything has been designed tastefully and uniquely, which gives you a feeling of a modern paradise on earth. Unimaginable extravagance in the marble floors, elegant furniture, and the antiques in each and every room of the house, exudes the richness, beyond one's imagination. Bill's house is furnished with profusion, elegance and with exquisite and eclectic taste. The house has a surfeit of extraordinary luxuries, in its most elegant form, imbuing the house with warmth and comfort. Entire house thoroughly clean, bright, and burnished. Bill still has his hundreds of luxurious cars, a helicopter that is parked at the backyard of his house. The house is having veritable cornucopia of modern and glamorous amenities. There is no end to Bill's richness. Bill has all the luxuries, which people could not even dream, to have in one life.

The session starts with a nice coffee. After the coffee, Bill gets up and Steve follows him through the sprawling house to a huge library with plethora of books, full of a vintage selection, but every book still in its pristine condition. There is a cozy overstuffed sofa set where one can sit and relax oneself. The wooden ceiling and the classic décor bring in just the right amount of quaint atmosphere to the room. From the French window, one can have the glimpse of the beautiful garden with colorful roses and tulips, and also feel the warmth of the sunlight, inside the room, through the beautiful, elegant curtains. It's a perfect place to relax and read.

However, Steve's attention goes mainly towards the books, which he knows are just show pieces and Bill must have not read, a single one of them.

He says to Bill, "It seems your library is just like your garden. You have hundreds of beautiful flowers, but you never took their fragrance."

Bill smiles and says, "I read a few, but not very thoroughly, mostly in a desultory fashion. After seeing these books and having no time to read them in my entire life, now I feel, how illiterate I am."

Bill and Steve sit in the library. There is pin drop silence.

Bill talks to Steve about their childhood days, spent in their village. He spends hours recollecting the memories of their childhood life, the beauty of their village, the large expanses of green fields, the lovely sunshine, the beautiful woods, the petrichor emanating from the fields, the earthy smell, the clear benign sky where you could count stars. Life which was full of contentment and happiness, far from the hustle and bustle of the urban civilization. The beauty of the nature, which could be experienced by seeing the trees, flowers, mountains, meadows, streams and those sylvan solitudes, farmlands, cattle, the bucolic landscape etc.

The favorite spot of Bill and Steve was a small rivulet, half a mile from their school. Beyond the rivulet, lay acres of grassland and hills, where Bill and Steve used to enjoy the natural beauty of the pastures. There was peace and serenity and a small abode of happy people. How simple and beautiful it was. A nonchalant life. Bill becomes quite nostalgic, remembering the pleasant old days.

Bill spends hours on this. Steve listens to him carefully. Sometimes it is good to recall the sweet old memories of life, instead on dwelling on a dark future.

Steve realizes among all human beings, there are two types of people, who seem to be struggling and suffering both. They are poor people and the old people.

Poor people are not the ones, who lack money but the ones, who have a lot of money, but their money is useless to resolve the basic problems of their life.

Old people are not the ones, who are retired and now nearing or surpassing their life expectancy, but the one who are restless and see absolutely no hope in their future. Bill now seems to be poor and old both.

Before Steve could start speaking, they are called for lunch.

The lunch is served with pure, delicate flavors, fresh ingredients, and flawless presentation. There are several dishes served for Steve. The food is scrumptious. Bill is very courteous, and Steve can feel his unstinted hospitality.

They finish their lunch and once again come back to the library.

Bill realizes that he did not allow Steve to speak and almost half the day has passed. However, Steve is never too keen to speak. Now Bill is quiet and asks Steve to start his conversation. It seems now Bill is ready. His mind is now clear. Bill has made space to listen and understand.

Steve starts his conversation with a small story.

He says, "Bill, this story is about "**One thing with which we play every moment and throughout our life.**"

Bill says, "Very strange, what is that?"

Steve says, "Bill, listen to the complete story."

"In a small village, there lived a small boy, who was about six years of age. While going to the market along with his mother, someone gave him a small brochure. When the boy came home, he saw that there were bright photos in that brochure, showing a gathering of large number of people, colorful shops, bright lightnings, a huge playground etc. The boy who had never seen any such thing in his life, feels amazed, runs to his mother and asks, "What are these photographs about, Mom?"

The mother replies, "These photos are of a massive fair, being held quite far from our village. The fair is very huge and millions of people from other villages and cities, converge in large numbers for fun and amusement. The fair has hundreds of outlets; there is music, dance, food, shopping, games, and other colorful events."

Listening to this, the boy gets tempted and expresses his desire to go to the fair.

The mother gives her son a portentous warning that in this massive fair they could be separated. Hence, she refuses by saying, "The fair is very huge and very crowded, with great hustle and bustle. God forbids, in case if you get lost, there is no chance I can find you back. I cannot take the risk of losing you at the cost of some momentary entertainment."

However, the boy pleaded again and again and finally got his mother to agree.

The mother said, "I will take you to the fair, but I have one condition."

The boy asked what it was, and the mother replied, "In the fair I will walk in the front, escorting and making way for you and you will walk behind me holding my mantle tightly, with both your hands. In any case, you will not loosen your grip. I will take you all around the fair and at last, we will come back home safely."

The boy assented and said, "Mom I will do, as you say."

The day came and the boy and his mother started for the fair. As they entered, the boy got mesmerized on seeing the glamour of the fair. There were large number of people including men, women and children wearing gorgeous, gaudy clothes and were beaming with joy. There was dancing and merry making. Drums were beaten and rustic songs were being sung. At some places, acrobats and rope dancers were showing their feats. At another place carrousel were crowded with boys and girls, men and women. The snake charmer was playing his flute pipe which was giving a melodious tune. In front of his flute, was a dancing serpent. All over the ground, stalls and kiosks had been set up. Some people were watching the tricks of the juggler and some of the magician. Bangle-sellers were having a brisk business with the ladies. The rope dancers, jugglers, magicians, and palmists attracted a huge crowd. They had roaring business.

Various cultural programs were going on there. Many women presented their folk dances. The sounds of the drums made the people in the audience, dance and sing. The people stood spell bound and enjoyed their feats. Everyone looked happy and gay. There was merriment all around.

The boy was holding his mother's mantle and was enraptured to see what he had never seen in his life before. Though the place was very crowded, but the mother walked circumspectly and made the way easy for the boy.

After some time in the midst of the fair, the boy saw some toy shops. The fair had toys galore. The toys were unique and never seen before. The boy called his mother from behind and requested her to take him to the toy shop. When he saw the variety of toys, he further got tempted to buy one.

He asked his mother if he could buy one, but she refused by saying, "If you buy a toy, how will you hold me?"

The son replied to the mother, "In one hand I will hold the toy and in the other, I will hold your mantle. Don't worry my grip even with one hand is very strong I will not lose you. Trust me."

The mother refused but the son importuned and finally got the mother agreed. The mother said, "Fine. I will buy the toy for you but be very careful. Don't lose your grip or else we will lose each other forever."

The boy smiled and said, "Don't worry Mom, I know."

The boy now got the toy. Now he was holding the toy in one hand and holding her mother's mantle in the other and they wandered in the fair. His grip was firm even with one hand.

After some time, the boy got tempted to play with the toy. Playing would not be possible, as he would have to use both his hands and he would lose the grip of his mother's mantle.

However, he thought atleast he could run the toy, by inserting and rotating the key. There was no harm in running the toy, which would hardly take few seconds. The temptation was so strong that the boy could not resist, and he reconciled himself, thinking, that he would lose the grip only for few seconds, and during that time he would keep a constant eye on his mother. Once the toy started, he would once again resume his grip and would follow his mother. He finally loosened his hand from his mother's mantle and started the toy. The moment the toy started, the boy got captivated and so immensely involved that he lost all orientation and time. He finally got involved in playing with the toy and forgot that he is losing his mother. In the pleasure of playing, he forgot his promise to hold his mother's mantle and eventually got separated from his mother.

Basically, all sensual pleasures are momentary, and they lose their taste after some time. Hence when the pleasure of playing with the toy faded, the boy realized that he is missing something important. To his consternation, he realized that he has reneged his promise and lost his mother. The boy started looking for his mother, but unfortunately there was no clue of his mother in the fair, where there were millions of people, and no one was concerned about anyone's problem. Everyone was totally absorbed in enjoyment. The son was stranded and left alone. He wandered all around the place frantically but could never meet his mother again. Same was the situation with his mother, who lost her son, as she found there was no one behind, after exiting the fair. The mother and the boy lost each other, forever.

The story ends here as an analogy representing the plight of human beings on earth.

The mother represents God and the boy is like every human being on this Earth. This world is like the fair, full of mesmerizing beauty, variant colors having all the glamour, plays, music, dance, toys, fun and frolic and all human beings are totally trapped in all the momentary pleasures, forgetting their origin.

When God created the world, the purpose was to experience it and enjoy it rightfully and finally come back to the origin. The primary objective was to stay connected with Him, and let God make the way, at every moment and every instance for us, in this mysterious world. Unfortunately, we human beings, just like the boy, got involved with the toys of this world, and disconnected ourselves with God. We got distracted by the ephemeral glamor and beauty and indulged into the momentary pleasures of this mortal world. Eventually we wander with all the pains and sufferings, having no clue of our actual destiny. This is the story of every human being on earth today, living a directionless and disoriented life."

Bill is listening very avidly. Before Steve could finish, Bill interrupts and says, "Steve I don't completely acquiesce to your analogy. I find your story slightly incongruous to the facts."

The question raised by Bill is as follows:

"I agree that the boy is too small to find his mother and so the mother has her limitations to find her son back in such a massive fair. However, in case of human being and God, God does not have any limitations. He is omnipresent and omnipotent. If He wants to find someone what restricts Him. Nothing in this Universe can restrict God if He intends to find someone. So why God does not come to the human being, finds him, resolves all his problems, and takes him back home. It's so simple."

Steve replies, "Bill your question is of great wisdom. I agree that God is omnipotent, and nothing can stop Him to reach anywhere. You are correct. However, there is a small deviation in case of the boy in comparison to the human being. The small boy is innocent and out of ignorance he gets tempted to the irresistible pleasure of the toy. It was a momentary act which distracted him for few minutes, but his immense love for his mother restores. He now recalls his mother and looks everywhere to get her back.

In case of human being, it is the other way round. God is looking every moment for human being and waiting when he would call Him and He shall run to rescue him. Unfortunately, whole life passes, God awaits, but human being does not recall God. The only thing every human being has taken for granted in life is "God." He is least interested in God. He has no concern for God. God is our last priority. God is the last chapter of our life or sometimes the missing pages in our books."

Bill asks curiously, "Why is that Steve?"

Steve answers, "Bill there are two basic reasons for this:

1. **Human being has no love for God.**
2. **Human being is all the time busy in toys."**

On listening the answers, Bill has further questions now.

Bill says, "Steve to some extent you are right, but I don't completely agree to your point."

Bill shares one of his experiences he had in the morning.

He says to Steve, "It is not true that people don't love God, or they have forgotten Him. I can give you a live example of my assistant, which I came across today morning. Her name is Sophia, and she is a very pious, earnest lady. She loves God, she goes to the church every Sunday, she remembers Him, and she has a keen desire to meet God. In the morning she expressed her feelings to me. I will call her and it's better if you listen to her directly. She also has a question, and I don't know whether you will be able to answer her or not. I am sure after meeting her, you have to change your perception."

Bill lifts his cordless phone and calls Sophia.

Sophia comes and Bill introduces Sophia to Steve. Sophia has been working with Bill since last ten years.

Sophia is already aware of Steve. Bill has been talking about Steve so many times, especially when Bill missed him a lot. She knows Steve is a deeply knowledgeable person and an old friend of Bill.

Bill tells Sophia about their discussion and asks Sophia to repeat the same question, she has been asking in the morning. Sophia is also very keen to have an answer.

Sophia says, "Hi Steve, Good morning."

Steve replies very courteously to Sophia, "Good morning, Sophia, how are you. What disturbs you about God?"

Sophia is a blunt lady, and she comes to the point straight away asking Steve, "Steve are you really willing to answer my question? I bet no one can."

Steve replies humbly, "I will try."

Sophia asks, "Steve tell me one thing. Why is God so adamant? Why has He hidden himself somewhere out of our reach? I remember God, but there is no response from Him. I want to see Him, but He does not show anywhere. I pray fervently, but He seems to be either busy or ignorant about my prayers. I am indeed doing all this, from the core of my heart, but I don't see any response from Him. Why has God concealed himself into the curtains, putting veil around Him? Why is God on a mute or silent mode?"

Sophia's questions seem to be a baffling one. After listening to her, Steve is speechless. He becomes totally silent and replies, "Sophia, I understand your question but right now I don't think it is the right time to answer. I need more time to discuss this matter with you. May be after a couple of days we will discuss this matter and I will try to give you an appropriate answer."

Sophia being a blunt lady replies, "Fine Steve, I already said, you will never have an answer. I know very well, no theories in this world can answer this basic question. However, search for a proper reply, prepare yourself, and come back if you have a logical explanation or else forget it. Don't bother yourself much. I am also not that ignorant about God, if there was a proper answer, I would have figured it out, myself."

Steve is very courteous and replies, "OK Sophia."

Bill sees all this and is surprised to see that Steve has chosen to remain silent on this question. Bill looks at Steve and he sees all the confidence of the world in his personality. Steve looks unabashed. Though Sophia may construe Steve's silence as his inability to answer the question, but Bill knows Steve is a stoic and imperturbable personality and there is a reason for him to be silent. Bill is aware that Steve has the answer but right now he does not intend to answer the question. Probably Steve deems it prudent to be silent.

Bill becomes more curious to know the reply, but he wonders when that time will come.

A little later, the Chef comes in and it's time for a small coffee break. After the break Steve has to leave for some other appointment. Also, it has been a long day with Bill. Steve takes leave of Bill. Though Bill wants the discussion to be continued but Steve has a commitment elsewhere. However, the next day, which is Friday, there is a national holiday, and then there will be the weekends. Even though Bill wants Steve to be with him, but he understands that he cannot command Steve now. He has to respect Steve and his priorities.

Hence, he says, "I don't want to disturb you on these holidays Steve. Please enjoy with your family. We will meet again on Monday."

Steve replies, "Thanks Bill, I will see you on Monday."

The manager comes to escort Steve in the sprawling house and takes him at the back side, where a chauffeur driven S-class Mercedes is ready to take him back home. Steve's home is in the adjoining city, hardly 150 miles from Bill's house.

Bill is back to his room. He feels much better today. Reminiscing the old days with Steve was very rejuvenating. While talking to Steve, he feels very relaxed.

Bill spends these three days at home. Bill notices a good change in himself, in these three days, having spending quality time with Steve. He feels energetic. He feels much better. He feels as if he has found something that he had lost long back. He feels, as if the emptiness within him is now filling up. He feels transfer of some positive energy towards him, the anxiety of declining health seems to be fading away. The fear of death is abating. He feels as if some miracle has begun in his life. First time he does not feel tired. It seems as if some heavy weighing stress and tension of decades, lying in one part of his mind, has been released. The hopelessness, which was disturbing, has just vanished. He found a new stream of energy within him. He feels as if he is reborn into a new world. A world where there is wisdom, happiness, and meaningful purpose.

After spending the weekends, Bill is now excited to see Steve, on that bleak Monday morning. Bill is eagerly waiting in the vestibule.

As promised Steve is once again back on the exact time. Bill is very impressed. A delay of even one minute would have made Bill restless. However, Steve has always been very punctual. He is never late even for a minute.

Bill asks, "Steve you are always on time. What is the secret of your punctuality?"

Steve says, "Punctuality is the first sign of discipline. I value time in my life. Bill, you know why Swiss companies manufacture the best watches in the world?"

Bill says, "Because of technology?"

Steve replies, "No Bill, technology came later. Primarily, because the people of Switzerland valued time. Valuing time, was there in their culture. Long back in Switzerland the sign boards on the highways did not mention the distance in miles. They mentioned it, in hours and minutes. For e.g., if you were to go towards Zurich, the sign board would state, "60 minutes to Zurich, the next sign board would mention 45 minutes, the next 30 minutes and so on. They evaluated everything in time, and they valued each and every minute and second. Hence, they became the best manufacturers of watches because they know the value of time.

Bill, we have limited time and energy. However, the resources in this world are abundant and infinite. Hence, we should value time so that with this limited time and energy, we can get the best out of the unlimited resources available in this world. I value each and every second and every minute of my life and I also respect the time of others, hence I don't fail in my commitments, unless and until they are beyond my control. Being late is disrespectful and insulting to others."

"You are right Steve," says Bill.

Steve further continues.

"However, Bill, despite all this, we should understand that now we are living in an extremely dynamic world. Today, things change abruptly, and they shift our priorities, unheralded. Now we have cell phones, emails on our mobiles, WhatsApp messages, and plus we have tied ourselves 24 hours to this enigmatic world. Hence sometimes it is difficult to maintain sharp timing for everything. It can unnecessarily increase our stress. Understanding this fact, we need to plan all our task very methodically and diligently and sometimes sharp timing may not add beauty but more stress and anxiety. Sharp timing is good for public services like flights, buses, trains, medical services, movies, board meetings, public programs, but when it comes to us as an individual pertaining to our daily routine work, I think we need to have a small adjustment factor. This adjustment factor will take care of all the contingencies that are beyond our control."

Bill says, "You are right Steve. It is not the bullet which can kill anyone, it is the speed of the bullet that causes the damage. In today's competitive world, we all are working at an unrelenting pace. It is not the work but the speed of the work that is more perilous in this fast moving and competitive world.

I agree with you Steve, sometimes sharp timing in every event throughout the day can cause unnecessary anxiety. Hence, we should plan our work methodically and give a commitment sensibly."

As usual Steve has his coffee with Bill, and they share what they had done in the last three days. Bill is curious to know what Steve does. Well as usual, Steve reads a lot of books, and he is an author of more than one hundred books. Most of his books have been one of the best sellers.

Bill still asks Steve, "What do you do most of the time?"

"I learn, this is the activity which I never stopped in my entire life. I still continue doing it. I love learning." replies Steve.

Suddenly there is a knocking at the door. Bill sees through the glass door, it's Sophia asking for his permission to come in.

Bill beckons her to come inside. Sophia is right there terminating the conversation.

Sophia says, "I am sorry to interrupt both of you, but Bill I need three days leave, next month."

Bill is surprised, as already Sophia had these three days off and she wants additional three days leave.

"What's the issue?" asks Bill.

Sophia smilingly replies, "Me and my husband are planning to go to the idyllic countryside next month, for excursion. We would be spending three days together. The idea just came yesterday, as my husband has been proposed a good holiday package from one of his friends. I have to confirm to my husband by today afternoon, to avail an early bird discount."

Bill says, "OK fine Sophia, I have no choice to refuse and disappoint you. Enjoy with your husband."

Sophia becomes very happy and says thanks to Bill.

Meanwhile Steve asks, "Sophia you seem to be very happy today."

Sophia replies smilingly, "Yes indeed."

Now Steve asks Sophia, "Sophia if you have five minutes I have one question for you, provided you are ready to give me a candid answer."

Sophia says, "Ofcourse Steve, you can ask me anything and I have no reservations to give you an honest reply."

So, Steve asks, "Let's say, if an angel comes from the heavens and says, that he would fulfill your three wishes, can you share with us what actually your wishes would be?"

Steve repeats, “Sophia I would really like to know, what actually you wish in your life, and not a dubious answer.”

Sophia looks very strangely at Steve and says, “Why not, it’s a simple thing, Steve, I can share it with you candidly.”

Steve asks Sophia to write those wishes on a piece of paper. Sophia takes a pen and paper and list those wishes as under:

1. Right now, I have a two-bedroom apartment. I wish I could have a three bedroom one.
2. My husband does not have his own office. I wish my husband would have his own office rather than a rented one.
3. I wish to go on a world tour with my husband seeing all the beautiful places in this world.

Steve once again asks Sophia, “Sophia are these really your first three wishes?”

Sophia confirms, “Ofcourse yes, Steve!!!”

Steve now asks, “Sophia where is God in your list?”

Sophia, who has no inkling regarding the purpose of the question, gets quite confused and asks, “Steve, I don’t understand, what do you mean by saying where is God in your list. You asked me to list down my three wishes and so I have. What has this to do with God now?”

Steve says, “Few days ago you asked me a question, why is God so adamant. Why has He hidden himself somewhere out of our reach? I remember God, but there is no response from Him. I want to see Him, but he does not show anywhere. I pray fervently, but He seems to be either busy or ignorant about my prayers. Why has He concealed himself into the curtains, putting veil around him?”

Steve further says, "Sophia if you remember God from the core of your heart and want to see Him earnestly, why is He not there in your priority list?"

Sophia is completely astounded, and she recalls the matter and her question to Steve. She was not expecting Steve to come with the reply like this. This was something out of the blue. However, she now understands what Steve means to say.

Sophia totally baffled says, "Oh my God!! Steve, I never thought in this way. Your answer has come from a very different perspective. You got me trapped into my answer."

Steve says politely, "No Sophia, I have not trapped you into your answer, but on the contrary, we all are trapped into our desires, and we have forgotten God completely. We remember God only when we have problems or unfulfilled desires. In normal course, God is nowhere in our life. Our desires are our priorities and not God or I would say everything else in our life is important like our family, business, friends, relatives, gadgets, and I am sorry to say, even our pets have a higher priority. Hence it is not God who has concealed Himself, it is human being who is running far away from God, being obsessed with his desires, emotions, and his greed to make more and more. Unfortunately, when these things do not help, we seek God. We are not true seekers; we seek God only when we have some unfulfilled desires or when we are suffering in life. That's the whole point."

Sophia now smiles and says, "Steve you are right. That day when I came to you, I had some personal problem in the morning, which seemed insurmountable. I was really disturbed. Hence, I was incessantly praying to God. I was so impatient that I wished, God would appear instantly and within a fraction of second, He would resolve all my problems. However, in the evening everything sorted out, on its own. Soon after that I forgot God completely. I forgot my questions also. I was then busy in my life as usual and as you rightly said my priorities changed. In these last three days I don't think I had anytime wished to meet God, so intensely. On the contrary I was dreaming about my pleasure jaunt with my husband, all the time. I do agree with your point. It is not God who is on silent mode or mute, but we human beings who are so entangled into our desires and daily routine, that we have consigned God to oblivion. It is only when we are in pain or we want something from God, we remember Him or else not."

Sophia pauses for a moment and asks, "Steve I want to ask you one thing."

Steve says, "Yes Sophia, please ask."

Sophia says, "Steve, do you think all the prayers of a human being are fulfilled by God?"

Steve replies, "Sophia, I cannot guarantee that all the prayers of a human being are fulfilled by God, but one thing I can say with certitude, that all the prayers of a human being are heard by God. Sophia, sometimes our prayers and our selfish desires sound the same and hence it becomes difficult for God to fulfill them, or else the world would become like a Hell. However, if a person develops the maturity to pray in the right manner, I guarantee, all his prayers would be fulfilled.

Hence, we need to pray with awareness, by discharging our selfish desires and motives and keeping a long-term view of this valuable life, which is on sole purpose to meet and become divine. If we pray with such awareness, then all our prayers will be certainly fulfilled. I hope you understand the point, Sophia."

Sophia replies, "Very well, Steve."

Sophia also seems to be quite impressed with Steve, she is all agog to become a part of the conversation between Bill and Steve, but she realizes Bill wants to have a tete-a-tete with Steve. Very reluctantly she leaves the room and resumes her work.

Steve says, "Bill I could have given the answer that day, but Sophia was not in the right state of mind. You can learn physics, chemistry and mathematics or all the worldly knowledge easily anytime but not the fundamentals of life. Just like molding steel, requires heating it to the right temperature, similarly to learn the basic truth about life, we need to have the right state of mind."

"What is that state of mind Steve. Can you expound on this subject?" asks Bill.

Steve replies, "We seek truth only when we are in pain, when we lose something valuable, when we are depressed with our failed potential and unfulfilled dreams, confronted by the uncertainties and exigencies of life. This is the irony of life, Bill.

That is why in Sikhism the Guru says, "**Pain becomes the medicine when comforts become the disease**." Our comfort zone makes us lazy; they make us addicted to bad habits, they make us slaves. Till the time we don't receive a kick, we do not wake up.

Bill, Buddha did not become a seeker when he lived in his luxurious palace with his beautiful wife. He became a seeker, when he saw an old person with a weak body, a sick human being and a corpse. On seeing these impending sufferings of life, which he would have to confront inevitably, Buddha, who was prince Siddhartha became restless and one night left everything in search of the ultimate truth of life."

Bill asks, "Steve I don't understand how come seeing an old person, a corpse and a sick man affected Siddhartha so gravely.

Everyone in this world sees this, yet it does not make any difference to anyone."

Steve replies, "Bill I agree to what you are saying. It was difficult for me also to comprehend; how did this affect Siddhartha so deeply. But then I realized that though Siddhartha was an adult, but his mind was pure and innocent like a child. Because of the prophecy made by the wise seers that the boy would either become a great king or a great spiritual leader, his father fearing he would become the latter, made sure that the prince lived a sequestered life of ease and luxury in the royal palace. So, he isolated him from the miseries and sufferings of this mortal world. He was raised in seclusion and kept away from the unpleasant worldly knowledge and reality.

Hence Siddhartha's state of mind was like a child. He was quite innocent and quite fragile too.

For e.g., if a small child sees some killing or any catastrophe how would he feel. You can imagine. The same happened with Siddhartha. The moment he saw these sufferings; death, decrepitude and disease, it was like witnessing a catastrophe for him. He was mentally troubled. He felt dismay, totally disillusioned and disappointed in life. The opulence of palace life no longer interested him, and he became curious to know the cause of all these sufferings.

Hence, he renounced all his worldly affairs in order to embark upon a journey of self-discovery and the ultimate truth.

Bill, people seek truth when everything fails in life. When our overwhelming desires, mental, physical, and spiritual troubles beset, we seek the truth in life. There can be momentary situations where people seek to know God, but it is an ephemeral state of mind.

If you ask me when a person matures, I would say when he becomes a true seeker of truth. Before that we are all children playing with toys."

Steve further adds, "Let me tell you one more thing Bill, while moving all around the world for the assignments that you gave me, I met hundreds of priests who must have done thousands of prayers, for people approaching them. I asked them what people usually ask you to pray for and unanimously all gave me the same reply."

"What was the reply, Steve?" asks Bill impatiently.

Steve replies, "They must have done thousands of prayers in their entire life for others, however in none of their prayers people desired God. People want more and more money, some want to have children, some want God to bless them with a boy and not a girl, some want to resolve their health problems, social problems, personal problems, financial problems, some want good job, some want promotions, some people want big houses, a big car, they want everything that exists in this world except one thing i.e., God. None of them ever asked to pray, that they want God.

Bill, we think, we love Him, but our love is based on our needs and desires. Till the time God fulfils our desires we love Him or else we abandon Him. Our love is conditional. So basically, we can't call it love, it's just a relationship of expectations, wearing a cloak of love. Ostensibly it seems that we love God, but the truth is that we are poles apart.

I hope you understand the point, Bill." Steve added.

Bill says, "Yes Steve I comprehend the issue clearly. You are right that God is awaiting human being to respond truly, but we all are indulged into this materialistic world and have completely forgotten Him. We are using God like an ATM machine.

We connect to this machine only when our cash goes down. I agree with you Steve. I am also a live example in front of you. I had the desire to become the richest man on earth. A few months ago, when I was asked to make a donation for a worthy cause, I took this opportunity to be seen as magnanimous and the biggest philanthropist in the world. Before I decided the donation figure, I compared it with others, just to show case myself, in front of the whole world, as the most pious man. The ostensible purpose was charity, but the actual aim was fame and recognition. I was so mean Steve; I regret it now.

Well Steve I understand your point, that we all just want to coax God, but we indeed have no affection towards Him.

However, Steve I am quite confused with one thing. How can we know whether we love God or not. I see so many people going to the temples and churches and everyone claims that they love God. Sometimes I have seen people crying while listening to the stories about God, but at the same time they behave vilely and display hatred towards people of other caste. I don't understand this phenomenon. How do we actually know whether we love Him or not. Is there any parameter to check love for God. Steve I would like to understand what true love exactly entail."

Steve replies, "Bill, this is a very complicated question. Even I remained confused regarding this matter and surprised while seeing people crying for God for a moment and within no time displaying hatred and atrocities with indignation towards innocent people of other caste. It took me a long time to resolve this question and find the right answer.

However, Bill, fortunately I got the right answers which I shall share with you.

Bill there are three signs of true love towards God. If you truly love Him, you will see these signs in one's Character. These signs are:

1. **God will automatically come in one's thoughts or in one's memory.**
2. **There will be an earnest desire to see God.**
3. **We will start seeing God in everything around us."**

Bill says, "Steve I don't understand these three points. I would appreciate if you can elaborate and clarify in detail."

Steve further elaborates the above points one by one:

He will automatically come in one's thoughts or in one's memory: "Bill, it is axiomatic, that if we want to remember God, we need some external support. Either we need to go to the Temple, the Church or the Gurudwara. We need someone to sing His songs, hymns or bhajans, we need someone to narrate nice stories about God, we need someone to glorify Him. Without external persuasion we cannot remember God.

However, in love we don't need external persuasion. For e.g., a boy who is in love with a girl, does he require any external source to reminisce her?

Does the boy need someone to tell stories so that he may not forget the girl, does he need someone to glorify the girl so that he should be able to recollect her memories? Does the boy need someone to sing a song to bring the spark and sizzle in their love? The boy and girl are so smitten with each other that none of these are required. The one you love will automatically exude from within yourself. The feeling of love is inexorable.

No external support or services are required. Your beloved will be there in your memory all the time, 24/7, 365 days. Just like your breath, love resides within you, breathing on its own. Love is self-propelling. It does not require any external agency, force, or power to make it happen. It happens on its own. The impetus of love with intense and potent emotions, evolves like a volcano from within yourself. It goes on, without pause, interminably. It will be beyond your control. It happens very naturally. It is very deep-routed, effortless and intrinsic. You cannot help it.

Hence when you love God, He will be there within you all the time. Even if you want to take him out, you cannot. It doesn't matter what circumstances may befall, but your love and devotion towards God will be unwavering and inextricable. If this happens then consider that you are in the first stage of love with God.

The second point Bill.

There will be an earnest desire to see Him: This will be the second stage of love. As you are aware, God is the last thing we want in our life. We never have a desire to see Him or to have Him with us. During our pleasures and joyful days, we are more concerned about our friends, family and relatives. For e.g., if you don't find your mobile phone how restless you become. If your friend tries to avoid you, how agitated you feel, if your girlfriend does not come with you on a date, how surly and disappointed you become. Do we have a similar concern about God Bill?"

Bill replies, "No, not at all. We have no concern for God. Our love for God is exiguous."

Steve continues, "Bill, if we ask people, how many times did they go to the holy places with a sole purpose of meeting God, rather than completing a formality or routine, or may be for fulfilling their selfish desires or for seeking heaven after death. The answer would not be encouraging.

However, in the second stage there will be an earnest desire to meet Him. This desire will be on your top priority list. To meet God, it will be your first and last wish. Nothing else will matter to you more.

Bill, it is not, that there are no expectations in Love. There is always one expectation i.e., Love demands company. Love does not demand pleasure, but it does demand for an everlasting companionship. It is the attraction that demands pleasure but love just wants you to be in the shadow of your beloved one.

When we are in love, we want our beloved to be with us. The most painful moments are when you are separated, or you have lost your beloved one. A person bereft in separation feels utter desolation in life. The pain of separation is overwhelming. You will feel sad, depressed, perhaps numb and lost. This loss can take over your thoughts and emotions and you will most certainly experience grief with a void in your life. There will be intense sadness and emptiness within you. Your emotional energy will totally vanish. Mentally you will be a broke. Your body will be in turmoil. There is no other pain more remorseful than the pain of separation in love. Hence the moment you fall in love with God, you will have this intense desire to see Him, to meet Him and to have Him all the time in your company. Nothing will bring solace except God's presence. Till the time this desire does not arise, love has not transformed into the second stage.

The third point Bill.

We will start seeing God in everything around us: This is the third stage of Love. You will see God in every human being, in nature, even in the rocks.

When I was in India, I had an argument with one of the Indian philosophers when I said, "You worship everything, you worship mountains, you worship trees, you worship rivers, you worship animals, planets, and a lot more. I don't understand the concept of your religion."

He gave me a very straight forward answer.

He said, "The concept of our religion is to see God everywhere and in everything. He is there in nature, in animals, in plants and trees, in every human being, He is there in the entire Universe. Everything, what we see in this whole Universe is a manifestation of God. The concept is to see God everywhere, so that we respect His complete creation. Till the time we do not respect His creation we won't be able to realize God."

Hence Bill, when we love God, we will start seeing him in our enemies also. We will have compassion for our enemies too.

In love with God, you get integrated with the whole world, the whole humanity, nature, and universe as if you are one with everything.

This oneness does not discriminate anything, be its people, nature or objects. It does not discriminate people on the ground of richness or poverty, whether they are good or bad, saints or sinners, friends or foes, beautiful or ugly, low caste or high caste, by their religion or by their color etc. Everything comes under the same purview, as it comes, for our ownself. You feel connected in harmony with everything in existence, at every level, by all means. This is the ultimate stage and we recognize such people as saints. Such people will not then cry on listening stories about God and then spread hatred, out on the streets.

This is the final stage of Love with God. Very few people get transformed into this last stage.

Till the time, we see others as others, we find them inferior, we find flaws in them, we discriminate them, we are far away from realizing God.

Hence a person in third stage, will be more understanding and altruistic. He will not be able to hate anyone, not even his enemies. A person who has transformed into true love of God will not have any hatred or enmity with anyone. The moment you sit with such a person you will feel unified with him. You will feel the divine in his company. You will feel peace, security and serenity with him. You will feel the presence of God in his Character. The emotions of such a person will culminate into eternal love and he will become love himself.

I hope you understand Bill," asks Steve.

Bill replies "Yes Steve, I got your point. We all talk of love, but we are poles apart from understanding what true love is. We are near to religious places, near to the various idols of God, but actually far away from God. We don't have a long-lasting relationship with God. Our relations are evanescent.

However, Steve, it is difficult to find such a person. Such person might be one in a billion.

Most of the people who believe in God, believe so, for the basic reason that they seek security and forgiveness. I have seen people reading the holy scriptures, but they do not do it for edification, but as a formality. You will not see a single word of the holy scriptures being implemented in their behavior or character. I am sorry to say the more they love their God, they carry more prejudices in their heart, hating people of other caste and religion, hence they become more insular and censorious. They read through their egoist mind, and they are unable to assimilate the true meaning of the scriptures.

Moreover Steve, there is a world of difference between what the true messengers or the prophets said during their time and the way hypocrites are misinterpreting on their behalf now, claiming it to be holy."

Steve says, "You are right Bill. That's exactly the point. Unfortunately, the common man who lives under his own guilts and fears, struggling for the basic needs of life and sometimes craving for the heavens in his next life, does not have the courage to distinguish between what is truly right and wrong. He becomes a victim and waste his entire life, under the influence of such fanatics and hypocrites, who have misinterpreted the total theory of religion."

Bill interrupts and says, "Steve not only religion but there are so many barriers in this polarized world like our nationality, our color, our caste, status, money, education, even gender, that it is impractical to consider a person of another sector as God. Moreover, our ego, so deeply entrenched within us, disintegrates us from our loved ones, our wife, our children, our parents, our friends etc. Hence to see God in everything is just like asking a blind man to see light in every moment of his life. Something impossible. Steve all these barriers have made us blind, completely blind, blind and blind!!!"

Bill continues.

"Steve, there is a world of difference, to what you are saying and what is actually happening.

I do espouse to what you are saying, but it seems like a utopia, someone rare would lead to this stage. To become as you say, is not everyone's cup of tea."

Steve says, "Fine Bill, now let's return to our original topic from this degression."

Bill says, "Fine Steve, the first point that human being does not carry any love for God and has no desire to see Him is now clear to me. Please clarify the second point. Human being is busy all the time in playing with toys and does not have time to comprehend the reality of this life."

Bill further says skeptically, "I never play with any toys Steve!!! Have you ever seen me with any toys. I don't get your second point."

Steve replies, "This is the irony of life Bill. The boy that I mentioned in the story earlier, was innocent and had only one toy. As soon as he got bored from that toy, he recalled his mother.

Unfortunately, we human beings are engrossed in thousands and millions of toys in our entire life, and we do not remember God. The toys do not let us come out of this trap and it's a frivolous waste of time. One after the other, we are always gripped in the desire of various toys and their addictions. Unfortunately, we are playing incessantly with those toys, from the time we were born and until we die."

"What is that toy?" asks Bill impatiently.

Steve replies,

"The toy with which human being plays all his life is "**THOUGHTS**."

When we are small, we play with toys like small cars, barbie dolls and other toys made of plastic and clay. However, as we grow up, our mind starts playing with "**THOUGHTS**." Our mind is twenty-four hours playing with this toy. The mind is inundated with unbridled thoughts all the time.

It is said, that man cannot live without air for more than one minute, two days without water and you can't survive more than eight days without food.

However as far as our mind is concerned, it cannot survive even for one second, without thoughts. If you try to stop your thoughts, your mind will become an insurgent, making you more restless and uncomfortable, just like taking a fish out of the water. The more you struggle with your mind, the more aggressive, it will become against you.

Bill, can I ask you to try one technique to evaluate how much control you have over your mind?"

Bill asks, "What technique Steve. Do you really have a technique to check how much control I have, over my mind?"

"Yes, ofcourse Bill," replies Steve.

Once again Bill is curious and asks, "Please tell me."

Steve says, "Sit quietly for five minutes and let your mind be totally thoughtless. Just check if you can manage to be thoughtless for five minutes."

Bill says, "Quite interesting. Let me check."

Steve says, "Bill, I will leave you for five minutes. Be in solitude and try to see how much time you can afford to be thoughtless."

Bill says, "OK Steve. I will do it right now."

Bill now sits in a relaxed position and starts this exercise. He now tries to be thoughtless.

Steve leaves the room and goes to the garden. The garden is huge and exceptionally beautiful with exotic plants. Roses abound in the garden. The enchanting flowers are blossoming with hundreds of colors. The delightful fragrances that drift through the air, the sound of birds and the tinkling of wind chimes, are really soothing to the mind and body.

Steve starts enjoying in the garden and wants to spend more time, but the exercise is only for five minutes. After five minutes

Steve goes back to Bill and asks, "So Bill, did you manage to become thoughtless."

Bill says, "Sorry Steve, forget about five minutes, I could not manage even for five seconds."

Bill once again seems to be quite confused and addled.

However, Steve says, "Bill, don't worry this is not only your mental condition but of everyone in this world. All human beings have the same problem.

This condition is just like parking the car in a safe and good place, but unfortunately the engine is still "ON." The engine never stops, generating more heat and noise all the time.

The biggest irony of human life is not that our circumstances are not within our control but it is the mind that has gone haywire.

It is quite easy to do all sorts of heavy exercises with your body. But this one simple technique on your mind will make you restless. I have asked so many people to carry this mental exercise, but everyone has failed miserably. They do it regularly, but they have admitted, despite all the efforts, some or the other thought does crops into their mind and they cannot help it. Mental relaxation is to make the mind totally thoughtless. This is what we call meditation.

Bill, we are so busy with various thoughts. Thoughts that are important for our daily tasks, thoughts that help us to achieve our goals, to learn and grow, thoughts that give us pleasure, thoughts that bring anxiety, worries, stress in life, thoughts that make us emotional, thoughts that make us what we are. We are all entangled into these webs of thoughts, interlinked and so badly mingled with each other, that they have become inextricable. They cannot be separated from us. They have complicated us, leading to more chaos and confusion within us. Every human being is internally lost into this muddle."

Bill interrupts and says, "I totally agree with you. Steve, you are going too deep now. You are getting exactly to the fundamentals. Our mind is nothing but a factory of thoughts. A factory which is running twenty-four hours, 365 days, without break, deteriorating and wearing out, day by day. Hence the mind is producing meaningless, unproductive, and unnecessary thoughts all the time, which has further gone, out of our control. You are right Steve."

Steve replies, "Bill before this matter becomes more complicated, let me simplify it. Let me delineate on this subject by sharing with you some more details. Let us understand what the sources of these thoughts are. Once we understand these specifics, we will have more clarity and understanding and once we have a better understanding, we can know how to make this prolific mind more peaceful, efficient, and productive.

So, Bill these thoughts occur basically due to the following five scenarios:

1. Pleasure.
2. Worries.
3. Activity.
4. Emotions.
5. Morals.

I will explain them one by one.

Pleasure thoughts: Dreaming that I am going to be rich, dreaming about being in love with a beautiful girl, dreaming about success in life, dreaming about materialistic things etc. are thoughts which give us pleasure. Things which we do not have in our actual life, we make them available in our inner world with the power of our imagination. All these thoughts are conceived within ourselves and we derive pleasure from them. This imagination is a thought process which we call fantasizing. People fantasize about things they intend to do, but they cannot do, due to their repressed wishes, their incapabilities, due to social stigma or various other reasons. Whenever we don't have any worries or any priorities or any activity to do, we get into the fantasizing zone. Especially at night we fantasize before we sleep. Men are quite promiscuous in their heart and fantasies. Sometimes when we wake up in the morning, the body is awake, but the mind is still in fantasizing mode and hence most of the people still lay on the bed. They lose all their energy. People become lazy due to fantasizing. This is the favorite toy of the mind; it wants to play with. No one in this world has power to refrain his/her mind, from deriving pleasure from this toy.

Worries: Worries are also thoughts, and they arise due to the following four reasons:

1. Uncertainties.
2. Responsibilities.
3. Assets and luxuries.
4. Attachments.

Worries come from uncertainties. Whenever there is uncertainty, worries will be the by product. Moreover, every human being born on this planet is confronted by the exigencies of daily life, hence worries are inevitable.

Worries are also associated with responsibilities. That is why children, young boys and girls, do not worry much because they don't have responsibilities in life, whereas parents worry more. Worries are a byproduct of responsibilities too.

People worry about their future, they worry about their jobs, they worry about their businesses, parents worry about their kids as they are attached to them. We worry about our health, our wealth, our circumstances, our future, etc. and there is no end to it. Worries are basically unwanted disturbing intrusive thoughts. Just like some person of unsavory character, residing in your house, without your permission, causing trouble to your health, family and future, so are these worrying thoughts. They dwell inside you, making you stressed and disturbing your inner world, thereby, having pernicious effects, by all means.

Further worries are directly proportional to one's luxuries and assets. If you want to count someone's worries, then count his luxuries."

Bill laughs on hearing this and says, "Steve this means I am the most miserable man on earth."

Steve says, "It is for you to examine. However, Bill worries are undesirable, uncontrollable and unacceptable thoughts. They entrap you causing significant distress. The more we try to get rid of them, the more intense they become."

Steve now comes to the next point.

Activity: These thoughts are required for our daily routine tasks. For e.g., driving car, to make food, to pay your bills, performing physical exercise, household tasks, day to day chores, etc. are the small activities for which we need our cognitive skills. However, for larger activities, i.e., to make your business run, an athlete preparing himself for the Olympics, a student preparing for the exams to become a doctor or an engineer or a lawyer, an author writing a book and trying to put more creative thoughts into his book, a story writer of Hollywood films trying to come up with a new story, a poet coming up with some new ideas, etc. These thoughts are called knowledge. We need proper knowledge to conduct these activities. These thoughts are important to lead a proper life but unfortunately these thoughts become a victim of our unbridled greed and ego, because of which we want more and more. Initially we want to become rich, then we want to become the richest man in the family, then the richest person in the city, then the richest in the country and finally the richest man on earth. The desire of excess materialistic things is a negation of inner peace and spiritual beauty. Hence these thoughts now make us restless, they make our life awful. These thoughts become the most perilous toys we play with, throughout our life. This is an endless and an interminable process.

Emotions: These thoughts arise due to good and bad feelings. Good feelings for e.g., love, friendship, compassion, forgiveness, contentment, etc. and contrary to that ill feelings give rise to jealousy, enmity, fear, hatred, pride etc. Emotions attribute to our thinking process. We all are controlled by our emotions and our emotions control our thought process. For e.g. when you are angry you lose your sensibility, when you envy or hate someone, you never intend to do good to them and in this process you harm your own integrity, when you are greedy you become corrupt, when you start comparing yourself with others who have more, you become restless, when people are obsessed with lust, they can become rapist or get womanized, when they get obsessed with ego they want to make their employees like slaves, when people get obsessed with their power or authority they can become cruel dictators. These emotions and feelings, all influence our thought process. All imbalanced emotions will put your thought process into a never-ending volcano, generating heat, causing a lot of restlessness within you and finally destroying all the good within you and make you a totally wretched man.

Morals: These thoughts give us the knowledge of what is right and what is wrong in life. They are important for us to become good human beings, but unfortunately, we hardly think of our actions on moral grounds. We bribe people, we speak lies, we cheat, we corrupt people, we fantasize immorally, we drink, we smoke, we humiliate our employees, we don't keep our commitments, we renege our promises, we do everything irrespective of whether it is good or bad to fulfill our selfish desires. What morals do we have in our life. Basically, we all are ready to go to any extent as long as we are not caught by law or by any other legal authorities.

Bill, most of the good people are not good because they have goodness within them, but because of the three basic reasons:

1. They did not get the opportunity to commit bad deeds.
2. They are already doing bad deeds, but the fact is that are not yet caught, and the world perceive them as good people.
3. They intend to do some immoral acts, but due to the social fear, they have refrained.

Bill, a postman could be considered very honest because there is no chance of taking bribes in his department but put him in a place where people offer bribes every day and see what happens.

Further Bill, I have seen a lot of spiritual leaders who were considered as God, but later they were convicted for crimes like rapes, murder, tax evasion, corruption. However, till the time they were not caught they were considered as angels.

Ask a person who is practicing celibacy, what goes into his mind. You can imagine, Bill.

In the corporate world, a manager, a CEO or a President, if he has young and a beautiful secretary, his behavior and attitude may seem to be very kind towards her, but if you actually check his thoughts, you will come to know, how unctuous and disingenuous he would be.

Goodness due to fear is no goodness. It is like light reflecting in a mirror and the mirror is perceived as the lamp. We all are mirrors, pretending to be good, but goodness is not within us. To cut the long topic short, we all rent goodness, we don't own it, Bill.

Coming to my original point, Morals. Basically, morality is the foundation of Character and Character is the foundation of a good society.

There are thousands of standards American, European, etc. for good products in this modern age. However, morality is the only standard to make good human beings. Making good products is a secondary task, one should primarily make oneself better. In this modern world we don't need better products, we need better humans. Hence have high morals and practice it, in every act of your life. This is the highest purpose of life."

Steve adds further, "Bill, by and large the mind is all the time busy in thoughts.

However, this process of thinking is an automated process. When we sleep, we feel that the mind is thoughtless, but it is not. The active part of the mind is thoughtless, but the subconscious mind is still thinking.

Thinking is an inexorable process in a common man's mind. Our mind is on a mental diarrhea. These huge quantities of thoughts pass through our mind so quickly we sometimes don't even notice it. Just like a person standing on a railway platform, bus station or at an airport terminal where a huge number of people come and go. They occupy us all the time and we do not get space to move freely. Similarly, these thoughts bind us, restrict us, limit us, imprison us, sometimes misleading us, getting disillusioned, leading to depressions, disappointments, and totally disoriented in life.

Sometimes, this endless flow of thoughts is tiring and exhausting. In order to draw the attention away from these thoughts, people eat and drink, take drugs, take pills or engage in vices, but this isn't the right solution.

There is a small incident, Bill. Once a man named Harry, on the first night of his marriage, was talking to his wife. They were discussing about their future on the bed. The wife was very talkative.

She asked, "Harry, this house is too small, we have only one room. When we have our first baby where will he sleep?"

Harry moved slightly away from his wife, made some space in between them and said, "See darling here is the space. Our baby would sleep here in between us."

The wife said, "Fine" but then she again asked, "When we have our second baby, then what, where would he sleep?"

Harry once again moved aside on the bed, made more space and replied blithely, "Darling, see there is more space, both the babies would sleep here in between us."

The wife said, "Fine but let's say if we have a third baby then what?"

Harry once again moved aside. This time there was no space, as he was on the edge of the bed, so he fell down. There was a huge noise and everyone in the house rushed to know what happened during the first night of this couple. Harry was lying down on the floor in agony. He was rushed to the hospital. He had a broken arm and a twisted ankle.

Moral of the story is, when we give space to unnecessary thoughts, we are bound to fall and invite pains and sufferings in life. Harry could have enjoyed his first night, instead he gave space to the unnecessary talks of his wife and broke his arm and leg. Our mind is like the garrulous wife in the story and when we give space to its unnecessary thoughts, we lose the good opportunity that life has given us to enjoy and live happily.

We can save our valuable time and energy, if we can reduce the number of unwanted thoughts. We can focus better if the unnecessary thoughts do not bother us. We can experience more inner peace, calmness and happiness if there was a way to stop all the unnecessary thoughts, which are meaningless and add nothing to our life.

Hence, all the time we play with this toy and miss everything meaningful in life, Bill.

Once we learn, how to stop playing with this toy, we will feel the abundance within us, we will experience the bliss, the ecstasy which is lying under the heap of our miserable unwanted thoughts. The thoughts which have anchored us and blocked our life, we have to leave them to feel the divine."

Bill is speechless but speaks in a low tone, "I agree with you Steve. Every human being on earth is entangled in the web of his own thoughts. Most of our thoughts are due to a sick mind which is on a mental diarrhea. The mind is excreting unwanted thoughts and unfortunately we are relishing it. Human being who was supposed to become the master of his mind is now a slave of a sick mind, which does not know how to think right.

Steve, I think I am imprisoned. My problem is not my physical health, it is my mental condition. Till the time I don't resolve my mental condition it will keep damaging my physical body. My thoughts sometimes burn me from inside. They make me sleepless at night and restless during the day. The most disturbing place in this world is within me. I cannot live with my ownself. Most of the time when I drink it is just to distance myself with my inner chaos. I agree with you Steve that when the inner world becomes like hell people start taking drugs, they consume alcohol, smoke, they binge on eating or drinking, or indulge into other sorts of pleasures. Till the time I am not free from my thoughts I won't be free from my circumstances.

Steve I would like to know further about our mind and how to control it."

Steve replies, "Bill I will continue with a new topic related to this subject in our next meeting and you will learn how to manage your thoughts. I think it's time to take your leave."

Bill seems quite calm, now. Before Steve leaves he says, "Steve first time I have expressed myself truly. I always feigned to this world as if I am the happiest man. I felt ashamed to admit that inspite of all the wealth I feel poor from inside.

However, after admitting the truth today, I feel better. I feel relaxed, I feel light. With you, now I see a small ray of hope. I look forward to a great noon in my life. The moment I met you, my worries seemed to be vanishing. I found new meaning to my life. I feel that the boy who got lost in the fair will be getting home safely."

Bill seemed to be quite sanguine now.

Steve holds Bill's hands and says smilingly, "What you believe will happen. Goodbye Bill. See you tomorrow."

Chapter 2

MIND

Steve comes back in the morning. Bill seems to be quite happy on seeing him. Today there is a new charm on Bill's face. Bill looks optimistic. He is not walking tiredly. His walking seems to be improving. Bill is looking more confident today. As usual they have coffee together and some handmade biscuits imported from Belgium. Basically, this is Steve's all-time favorite. The toasty sweetness and curiously floral aroma, make them awesome. Bill still remembers Steve choices and is taking utmost care of Steve.

Today Bill is more keen to listen rather than to speak. He urges Steve to start with his second story.

Steve says, "Bill this story which I believe originates from the Sanskrit literature, I heard from Osho – Acharya Rajnish, the Indian philosopher.

Once there was a nomad, travelling from one place to another. After a long and tiring walk, he saw a huge umbrageous tree with lush green foliage. The nomad sat beneath the tree. As he was quite tired, he thought of taking some rest. Soon the weather became cool and pleasant, there was fresh air and a complete solemn silence, the nomad lulled into a deep slumber. He woke up after couple of hours and he felt quite rejuvenated.

However, he felt very hungry now. He wondered if he could get some food.

By a quirk of nature, suddenly he saw a table covered with a white linen cloth, appeared miraculously on his right side. The table was having unlimited assortments of viands, several dishes with exotic aroma and garnished to augment the visuals, leaving the nomad, drooling helplessly.

The nomad who was famished, without wasting a second, started eating like a gourmand. The food was extremely delicious. After eating he felt thirsty and wondered if he could get something to drink. Soon there was cool water along with refreshing drinks and invigorating fresh natural juices on the table. The nomad guzzled all the drinks one by one.

After having a perfect meal, the nomad felt quite excited. He was totally overjoyed. It seemed as if it was his luckiest day. This was something out of the blue, something impossible that happened beyond his imagination.

He realized that something was peculiar with the tree. He again looked at the tree, except the thick green leaves dancing with the wind and few birds chirping on the branches, he found nothing.

Now having no inkling about the matter, he began to wonder, "How come all that I wanted got manifested into reality. Everything I wished under the tree since morning is getting fulfilled. I had a nice sleep, had a lavish lunch with the finest refreshing drinks. All that I desired, happened like a miracle."

He looked all around frantically but there was no one. He wondered what is happening. The moments became ominous now.

The nomad became quite suspicious since there was no trace of human beings anywhere. He wondered with trepidation, with a feeling of premonition now. However, grasping of everything that happened and after giving a deep thought, he finally concluded that there must be some unholy ghosts on the tree who could read his mind and fulfil his wishes.

The moment he concluded this; the ghosts appeared in front of him cryptically, starring at him belligerently. As he saw the ghosts, the nomad became hysterical, not comprehending why all this was happening. He started fidgeting around the tree with impatience. He got totally confused and thought that this was a trap, with some nefarious purpose and now he would be abducted and killed. To his shock, exactly the same thing happened. The ghosts abducted him and killed him. Unfortunately, the nomad died. The story ends here.

Now, the question arises, who were these ghosts and why all this happened. At one moment the ghosts were fulfilling the nomad's desires and at the next moment they were outrageously violent. Was it really the ghosts or something else. What is the reality of this story?

The truth is, it was not the ghosts that made all this happen, but it was the tree. The tree was basically a "Kalpwraksh" which means "The tree which fulfils all that you conceive and desire." In Sanskrit "Kalp" means what you imagine and "wraksh" means tree. So, a Kalpwraksh means the tree that fulfils what you think and desire.

Hence, all that was being conceived by the nomad under the tree, was getting fulfilled. When the nomad thought of taking rest, the tree made an appropriate environment for his rest, when he was hungry, the table with a perfect meal appeared, when the nomad felt thirsty, all the refreshing drinks were served, creating an atmosphere of elegant conviviality. Unfortunately, due to a feeling of fear and presentiment, when he thought negatively about the ghosts, the ghosts showed up and finally when he thought that the ghosts would abduct and kill him, so it happened. So, it was the Kalpwraksh which made everything happen, as conceived by the nomad.

Now the question is, "Is there really a Kalpwraksh in this world or this is just a fairy tale?"

"What do you think Bill?" asks Steve.

"I don't think there is any such mythical tree in this world, Steve. These is just an apocryphal story, all chimerical." replies Bill.

Steve says, "No Bill, this is not just a fairy tale, there is indeed a Kalpwraksh in this world."

Bill impatiently asks, "Where is it, Steve. Give me the location. Tell me the address. I would like to go there and the first thing I want is, to recover from my debilitating headache. I can give you all my wealth if you can give me the address of that Kalpwraksh."

Steve replies, "OK Bill, I will give you the address right now. Listen to me carefully.

Our "**Mind**" is that Kalpwraksh. It is our mind which makes things happen as we conceive and believe. We become what our mind conceives."

Bill is stunned, "Interesting Steve, please continue."

Steve continues and says,

"Bill, whatever you see in this world, is all a manifestation of one's thoughts. Anything produced by human being, was basically a thought at the first stage. The blueprint of everything made by man physically in this world, existed in our mind first. Whatever we see around us, like a small hair pin, different types of gadgets like mobile phones, laptops, television, toys, the colors, the art, the music, the clothes, the houses, the furniture, the cars, the trucks, airplanes, the roads, the buildings, the skyscrapers, or any engineering marvels etc. everything was basically in the form of thoughts in someone's mind. It did not come accidentally into its physical shape. It was all incepted by a thought.

The beginning of all that is manufactured by human being in this world, was just a thought in the form of desire, an imagination, a fantasy or probably an earnest need. It was then manifested by the mind. When it became the belief or an earnest desire of mind, human being through his hard work, intellect and using the external resources, gave it a physical form.

Hence mind is the Kalpwraksh, the tree that manifests what you constantly feed within it.

If our mind conceives positively, we will have positive outlook and positive aroma in our life. If our mind conceives negatively, we will encounter negativity in our life. A person with negative mind set cannot make his circumstances or life positive. So, basically, the mind manifests what we think firmly and believe."

Steve further says, "I hope you are getting my point, Bill."

Bill replies, "Of course Steve, I agree with you. I became the wealthiest man not by luck or by an accident, you know it very well. Right from childhood I had that earnest desire of becoming the richest man on earth. I totally agree that it is our mind that has the power to transmute all our dreams into reality.

However, Steve I want to know the most important thing, how to control our mind: such an important and a sensitive gadget."

Steve says, "Fine Bill, listen to me carefully.

Bill, Mind cannot be controlled. It is basically like a huge flow of thoughts, exactly like we have Niagara Falls with enormous water and all the water with gigantic current. Mind has infinite thoughts, and the pressure of these thoughts is beyond our control. If we try to control the thoughts, probably we will land up into a miserable situation. Hence, we must not try to control our mind but try to condition it. Just like an air conditioner, that conditions the air and does not control the air. It only takes out the heat from the air. Similarly, we need to take out the heat or the negativity from our mind and we will find our mind, in its right functions.

Mind can be conditioned by following three ways:

1. Positive thoughts.
2. Positive Environment.
3. Meditation.

Just like our body needs nutritious food, our mind needs positive thoughts. Bill let me tell you one thing. I experienced all transformation within myself only by positive thoughts and not by any of the religious austerities like fasting, taking bath in some holy river, giving money and asking some priest to please the Gods and Goddesses on my behalf, hanging a horseshoe on my door etc. I met so many people, who admitted that performing all these austerities and liturgies for so many years, left them finally unassuaged.

Only one thing helped to condition their mind and that is positive thoughts, whether they come from a spiritual book, a motivational lecture, from some quotes or maxims, didactic stories etc. Hence positive thoughts are the fundamental ingredients to condition your mind.

Well thoughts may not influence you all the time, hence you need positive environment also. Just like when you sow a seed in the soil which is fertile, but if the environment is not conducive, the seed may not germinate. Hence, we need a positive environment in which our mind becomes open and allow the positive thoughts to blossom."

"What exactly is positive Environment? Can you explain to me precisely Steve," asks Bill.

Steve replies, "Bill, there are lot of definitions for positive environment, but I would like to put it in a simple, concise and a clear form. Hence forth you will have no confusion regarding positive environment."

"Positive environment is, where all your five senses (touch, taste, sight, smell and hearing) receive positive inputs."

"Bill, when we go to an ashram, we feel there is some divine power. However, it is not the power, it is the simplicity and the purity, which our five senses experiences. We smell the pure air, we can see nature around us, the sky, the moon, the stars, we eat simple but fresh and organic food, which is nourishing to our body, we hear the divine thoughts without any distraction, we can sense the vibration of purity and feel it throughout our body, mind and soul. There is no miracle. This kind of environment affects our body very positively, our health and ultimately our mind. Hence, we experience a divine pleasure in such kind of an environment. We feel as if there is some supernatural power in the Ashram, but Bill, there is no supernatural power it is just the power of Nature that exists in abundance.

In today's world we are surrounded by an environment of gadgets, surrounded by people who are lost in their lives and making us confused, expectations from everyone, coming across the negative emotions like jealousy, hatred, enmity, fear, depression, glamorous faces with intense pain and loneliness within them, educated people without any awareness, wily opponents, surrounded by unbridled competition, negative news all around, uncertainty, a chaotic world, a hypocrite world, rapid changes in this commodifying world, a money oriented world, materialistic world, the world rushing towards nowhere, creating more mess and chaos all around etc. Hence Bill, when we experience the environment which is far from all these defilements, we feel peace. Moreover, when we are with Nature in its purest form, from which we are created, the clean air, the pure water, the clear sky, simple fresh organic food, we feel energized. We feel there is some divine energy in the Ashram, but believe me there is no such divine energy, it just has the type of environment, what our mind, body and soul need precisely.

I hope I am clear Bill."

Bill says, "You are right Steve. Very enlightening. A person of your caliber can only understand these intricacies, or else a common man cannot have the sapience to know the facts so precisely."

Steve continues, "Bill, now listen to me carefully. As far as this world in considered, whatever the situation may be, but we have to still live in this world. No matter how disoriented it seems, but we have no choice. We have to perform our role which is inevitable. We have our responsibilities and priorities. Hence physically isolating ourselves from such an environment may not be possible. However, we can mentally isolate ourselves from this environment."

"How to mentally isolate ourselves?" asks Bill impatiently.

Steve answers, "Bill there are five basic ways. The five ways are.

1. Consider your mind as the most beautiful place of the world, even better than the heavens in this Universe.

Don't put anything in this prolific mind, which contaminates it and makes it impure.

2. Become the owner of your mind. If you cannot master your mind, it's fine. But don't give your mind on rent to unnecessary people, so that they can store their cheap and disturbing thoughts in your mind.
3. Purge your mind with the guilts of the past, anxiety of the future and burden of the present.
4. Develop the wisdom to identify what is important and what is not important and develop the ability to avoid and ignore things, which are unimportant and unnecessary.
5. Maintain balance in life. Don't get obsessed with any thought, emotion or desire."

Steve says further, "Bill the most important place in this whole world is your own mind. Unfortunately, every human being on this planet is least concerned about it. All spiritualism is nothing but to condition your mind. With your mind, as I told before, you can have worldly success, you can have spiritual bliss or probably you can have both."

Bill says, "Steve. I agree with your point. We all are least concerned about our mind which deserves the utmost priority in our life. Unfortunately, in my obsession to become the richest man on earth, I ruined my internal world. I never knew that millions of dollars can also make someone the poorest man on earth. My mind has become a place where all the selfish people of this world make their stay, my mind is a place where all the greedy people are stretching and taking everything, my mind has become a place where all the worried people of this world come and start sharing their worries, it has become a place where a salesman pretending to be honest, good looking and handsome, is fooling me from within myself. What a pathetic place I am holding.

All these people sometimes cause a terrible commotion within me. All these sick people are nothing but my own different images Steve. They are my own different images, being extremely rowdy within me. My mind is in a whirl. I want to emancipate myself from the thralldom of these disturbing and perpetual images. I don't understand how to get rid of them."

Steve says, "Don't worry Bill. No one in this world, is a single entity. Our mind is poly-psychic. Physically we are one but psychologically we are multifaceted. We have a crowd within ourselves or I would say, we all have different versions of ourselves, within ourselves. Some versions are good, and some are bad. The bad ones are incompatible within us, with our soul, making us restless, day and night. However, we have chosen these versions. That is why the wise people say, don't do immoral things, don't cheat anyone, don't do injustice to anyone, be a good human being. This was all primarily for the well-being of your own. However, these versions are not real, they are only impressions. They will obliterate the moment you purify your mind, with the nectar of your awareness. So, Bill, don't worry, these impressions will never torment your heart, once you are enlightened."

Bill still speaks in a despairing tone, "But Steve I feel a kind of compunction and deep regret about my past. I think I have merely wasted my life into accumulation of materialistic things, which had no meaning, all zilch."

Steve speaks in a stentorian voice, "**Bill, don't make your mind a graveyard of your past guilts.** Let the bygones be bygones."

Steve lowers his voice and says, "Bill our mind is sometimes disturbed due to the trivialities of life, something which is insignificant, but our overthinking makes it intense, unnecessarily. The intense impressions and memories within our mind are just like a room filled with darkness from ages. However just like a small lamp which dispels the darkness within no time, so is awareness. It will obliterate all those impressions within no time. All your negative notions, no matter how indelibly they are imbedded, they will disappear as if they were never there. All anxieties, fears and insecurities will not dare to touch you Bill, once you have truly introspected yourself and you are awakened in life."

Bill says, "Steve, as I listen to you, your words penetrate deep inside me. Whatever you say, seems like divine words full of wisdom, which seems to be nourishing and enriching my soul. Steve, the day you started coming, I think I am gathering the strength to throw all these sick people out from my mind."

Steve smiles and says, "Good Bill."

Steve further continues, "Bill you need to do three things after I leave."

Bill asks surprisingly, "What are they Steve?"

Steve replies, "Bill, read atleast one to two hours a day and try to assimilate all the wisdom. You have a good collection of books."

Bill asks, "What shall I read Steve?"

Steve replies, "Acquire wisdom, leave away all the knowledge."

Bill asks, "What is the basic difference between knowledge and wisdom Steve?"

Steve replies,

"The one that binds and attaches you with this artificial and materialistic world is knowledge. The one that liberates and detaches you with this mortal and materialistic world is wisdom."

"Wow Steve. I never thought like this. You are great." says Bill.

Steve continues further.

"The second thing is Bill, you have a nice garden. Get up early and see the sunshine. Throw the painting of sunshine hanging in your bedroom, in an ornate frame. It is worthless. It is lacking the illumination that your body and mind needs.

Bill says, "Do you know the cost of that painting, Steve!!! I bought it for 30 million dollars. Are you asking me to throw it???"

Steve says, "Yes Bill. You see the sunshine in that painting every morning which is meaningless. That painting is only empowering your ego and nothing more. It is adding more poison in your life."

Bill remains silent for a while. He probably does not like Steve's suggestion and asks sarcastically, "By the way how did you know about that painting which is in my personal bedroom? You have never been to my bedroom."

Steve replies, "It is all over the social media Bill. All the exquisite paintings and artwork in your house worth millions of dollars are exhibited on the social media, a reckless display of your prodigality and your unconscionable spending. I am sure this must have been done with your permission only."

Bill smiles and is speechless.

Steve says, "Third, the most important thing Bill. In your entire life you have been accumulating wealth. Now stop doing it and start "**Giving**." Bill, start giving to this world, by all means."

Bill looks surprisingly at Steve.

However, Steve continues by saying.

"Bill, the fundamental of human existence is based on giving or else this world would soon become like a Hell. Giving basically elevates your self-esteem. A person with a higher self-esteem will be more confident, enthusiastic and will not get easily depressed or sad. The act of giving adds more beauty to your life and within this world.

Bill there is immense power in giving. When you give, you become a part of the benevolence of the Creator i.e., God. You become a team member of God. All messengers who came in this mortal world, had one common virtue in them i.e., they just gave everything they had. They accumulated nothing for themselves. They gave all their wealth, all their knowledge, their blessings, showered all their love and compassion without any discrimination to everyone, they lived every moment of their life just to give to this world. Bill giving is a spiritual act, it enriches your heart and soul, it empowers you, you feel wealthier day by day, you will have a feeling of fulfillment, you will feel close to humanity and Godliness.

Bill, giving is the first step in restoring your relationship with nature and God. Everything in this Universe is contributing, the sun, the stars, the moon, the sky, the rivers, the trees, the mountains, the rocks, our earth, the trees, the plants, the flowers, birds, animals etc. The key to harmony, peace and happiness lies in the quality of giving. Giving is an act of compassion which augments love, care and contentment. Not only it enriches your heart but provides transcendental peace and joy to your soul. Through giving you can make this world like Heaven.

However, Bill, while you are engaged in some eleemosynary activity, follow the five basic rules.

1. Give sensibly, with good intentions and with a large heart.

2. Give indiscriminately.
3. Give with humility.
4. Once you give, just forget it. Don't empower your vanity.
5. Give, as if you are an instrument in the process of giving and not the actual source.

Don't use the word donation. Like someone wise has said,

"No one is the owner of wealth. We all are just, trustees."

Bill is listening to Steve very avidly and says, "Steve, thanks a lot. You are right. I have just been accumulating all the wealth, all my life, meaninglessly. I think I have debased myself. I feel regretted now. I honor and cherish your enlightening suggestion. I am fortunate to find the right direction in my life."

Bill becomes pensive.

Well, the chef comes in and it's time for lunch.

Bill and Steve go for the lunch. During lunch Bill asks Steve to teach him meditation. Steve agrees. They return after one hour. However, Bill has an appointment with the doctor. The doctor has already arrived for Bill's regular checkup and is waiting in the lobby.

Steve accompanies Bill and they are now in the lobby. The doctor is performing the regular checkups and examines Bill's reports. Bill wants to say something, but the doctor is busy in examination. However, the doctor advises Bill to continue with his regular medicines and leaves.

As the doctor leaves Steve says, "Bill, change your doctor immediately!!!"

Bill asks surprisingly, "Why Steve, what happened?"

Steve says, "The doctor is not good!!"

Bill says, "Not good!!! Do you know that he is a nonpareil neuro-oncologist, considered to be the best in the world. He has an experience of more than 30 years. He has patented some medical instruments. He is the doctor of highest caliber in his field."

Steve says, "I don't doubt what you are saying, but still, he is not a good doctor."

Bill asks, "What makes you feel like that Steve?"

Steve replies, "Bill how do you judge a good doctor. Tell me?"

Bill says, "By his qualification, by his experience."

Steve says, "Bill, that is true but still this is not sufficient. In order to judge a good doctor, the fundamental rules are:

- **How much questions did the doctor ask you, about your health.**
- **How much did the doctor listen to you, about your health.**

For a good treatment, it is imperative, that the doctor gives more attention to the patient before giving his advises and prescribing the medicines.

Bill while the doctor was here, he neither listened to you nor did he ask you any questions. He just checked your blood pressure, your diabetes, few reports and then he asked you to continue with the same medicines.

Bill he may be a good doctor by his qualifications and experience, but not the way he is treating you."

Bill says, "I agree with you Steve. I also felt something inherently missing, but I am not enlightened like you that I could figure out so clearly."

Bill phones one of his managers and asks him to change his doctor immediately.

Bill says, "Steve I may change the doctor, but it is insignificant. What difference does it make. As such I am going to die and that too with a lot of sufferings. All these medicines and philosophies would just palliate my illness and distress but will not cure me."

Steve replies, "Bill, do what you can in the best interest of your health. Don't lose hope."

Bill laments, "Don't reconcile me like a child Steve. I know the truth."

Steve asserts and speaks in a stern voice, "Leave the worries of your future Bill. Everything will fall right, within its own course. As long as you are enjoying this moment in the right spirits, don't pollute your mind with unnecessary anxiety of future, guilts of the past or any burdens of your present. Purge your mind. Don't let your atavistic fears pulverize your emotions. Don't desecrate your spirit.

Bill, medical science has no clue about the vital forces of this Universe and cosmos, how it manifests through all space and life, its healing powers. You have no clue of it. Leave everything on its own. Don't interfere with the miraculous cosmic power within you, with your ignorance, with your inadequate intellect, with your erroneous beliefs or disbeliefs, with your narrow perspective, with things that apparently seems true, with your medical reports or the prognosis of your doctor, with your guilts or with your hopelessness, with your past or with your future. Just make yourself totally null and void. Remove your mental existence. Get absorbed in the present. Enjoy the moment without expectations, without stress, without worries of the future. Detach yourself with everything. Leave all your mundane ruminations behind. Stay quiet and stand firm. Be here in the present, be pure, be calm, be free and be nothing. Don't conjecture about your future. Submit yourself and feel the oneness with the ultimate. Try to become thoughtless Bill.

Bill, just meditate, meditate and meditate!!! and your body will rejuvenate, and your mind and soul will become divine like a newly born child."

Bill is totally speechless. He just listens to Steve and wants to listen more and more. The words seem to be divine. Bill is watching Steve.

Steve closes his eyes and sits quietly, probably goes into meditation. Steve's words spoken with such certitude, are resonating in Bill's mind, he closes his eyes too. The way Steve has spoken with conviction, his words influence intensely on Bill. Steve's fervent words entrance Bill and cause a complete black out within Bill. Bill's ruminations are fading, all fears, worries, guilts seems to be obliterating, there seems to be a vital energy in Steve's words. Bill feels good, as if time has stopped and there is no past or no future, only the present, as if nothing exists around him including his own physical body. Bill feels lighter and lighter as if he is floating in the air, in a state of oblivion. There are no thoughts, there is a peaceful sleep, a sedate state but every moment of this sleep is filled with exalted happiness, as if life has entered into some new horizon, the feeling is not coming from the five senses, as if some divine energy is touching the soul, making the entire inner world pleasant and calm, there are no words to define this experience.

After one hour Steve grabs Bill's hands and wakes him. Bill gets up and tries to figure out what happened. He remembers Steve's divine words and then getting lost in nowhere. It was almost one hour. No trace of anything, no thoughts, beyond the realms of time, totally mindless. Bill is astounded and cannot comprehend this experience. Well, whatever it was, it was a wonderful experience.

Now, it's time for Steve to leave.

Bill expresses his gratitude to Steve and with great courtesy says goodbye. He awaits Steve the next day.

However, Bill is surprised with the overwhelming experience which he cannot comprehend. It seemed like a moment of epiphany, experiencing the inner bliss. Its essence is still alive within him. It was like falling into an ecstatic trance. It was inexpressible, it was ineffable.

Chapter 3

MOTHER'S DAY

Steve comes in the morning as usual. Bill is sitting exuberantly in his garden with a little bonfire. Well, it's not that cold to have a bonfire, which makes Steve quite surprised, apparently. Steve goes and sits with Bill.

He asks Bill what he was doing.

Bill replies, "Steve, I am burning all those paintings as you suggested yesterday. You are right Steve, I used to see the sunshine in these paintings which just empowered my ego. These paintings are worthless. I feel much better today, as if I am burning my sickness."

Bill adds further, "Steve constructing this house was indeed foolhardy and unnecessarily ostentatious. There are eighteen bedrooms in this house, and you will not believe, almost fifteen rooms have never been occupied. It was a folly to construct such a big house. I wonder if spirits might be haunting the rooms now and sometimes me too.

It was my vanity and exacerbate greed to enhance the sense of self-importance. My house displays my sybaritic lifestyle and indulgent character. This all is pathetic. I was bound to become sick. There is no doubt."

Bill continues, "Steve, I felt lonely in this place. I started disliking my house. This house is like a museum telling the story of a man who started from his richness and now ending towards his sickness. I hated everything which I made, just to showcase my richness and elaborate my pride. However, the day you started coming here, there is a change in the aroma of this house. I wanted to leave this house and go to an Ashram. But now this house itself seems like an Ashram to me. I have started liking this place. Your presence has made this place divine."

Steve replies, "Bill everything which is in excess to your needs, is indeed worthless. Limit your needs, become minimalistic, and see how enjoyable life is."

Bill says, "You are right Steve. Excess also creates an imbalance in life. I have lost the ability to keep my life in balance. It is weighing too much on my mind now."

Bill continues, "Well Steve today there is a small function in our club. They are celebrating Mother's Day. I wanted to avoid it, but since I am the president, I have to be present and address the members with few words. However, Steve, you are supposed to give a small speech."

Steve asks, "Me? Why me Bill?"

Bill says, "Yes Steve you have to, because I want you to speak."

Steve is not prepared for an extempore, and it would be like fish out of water, but because of a strong insistence from Bill, Steve agrees.

As usual Bill and Steve have their breakfast and leave for the function at the club.

Bill's car is one of the most expensive cars, personalized armored BMW, a kind of a royal drive with opulent interior. Four other cars, all factory versions and heavily fortified, are escorting Bill's car. Soft jazz music is playing. Bill has got an exquisite taste for everything. Steve is quiet and enjoying the peaceful ride.

They are on the crossroads, while the lights are red. Suddenly a mud ridden beggar comes tottering towards Steve, a cadaverous face, old and feeble, hands outstretched and eyes brimming with expectation for some money or food. Steve looking to his deploring condition could not resist giving some money and starts rummaging through his pockets.

Bill seeing this immediately admonishes and speaks in a deprecatory manner, "Steve, what the hell are you doing?"

Before Bill could say anything, Steve rolls down the window and gives a ten-dollar bill to the beggar.

However, Bill continues, "Steve don't be so benevolent. These beggars are not beggars, they are wily imposters. Don't go on their frail and feeble condition. They act so, to make you feel sympathetic."

Steve replies, "Bill even if they are imposters what difference does it make by giving ten dollars to them."

Bill replies, "It's not about the ten dollars Steve. The point is, if the beggar misuses your money, let's say, drinks alcohol, takes drug or does any illicit act, you will be held accountable for his actions in the court of God."

Steve is surprised to listen to this and replies, "How come, this is possible? This is irrational."

Bill says, "Since you are the ultimate source of this money, hence you will be held responsible for the misuse of the money by that beggar. This is quite logical. Steve, you might be very knowledgeable, but what I am telling you is the truth."

"Bill, what you are saying, is apparently correct, but still this matter needs a rational cogitation. Well, we will deliberate on this topic some other day," says Steve.

Bill says, "Fine Steve, as you wish."

Bill and Steve finally reach the club. It is a sybaritic establishment, with a club house which is a magnificent edifice. Several people approach Bill with a friendly word of greeting. Bill returns the greetings with a nod, sometimes a smile or words of cheers and sometimes with a solemn expression. Bill reaches the club office. He is accompanied by his staff.

Very soon the function starts. Some small speeches are given by some members and now Bill is on the stage, finally.

Bill is a greatly confident person. Bill's personality exudes the aura of his wealth and power. He looks magnetic on the stage. Bill looks like a lion, fearless, intrepid, and bold. He stands like an emperor. To see Bill speaking on the stage is a different experience. Bill does not need any introduction and hence he starts by saying.

"Once a chartered accountant was given a balance sheet in which, there were only expenses and just disbursements. There were no profits or gains.

After studying the balance sheet, the chartered accountant asked his assistance furiously, "Are you insane, such a worthless balance sheet you have brought for my approval, with only expenses, no gains, no profits, no returns on the investments, total loss. What is this? Is this a joke? You expect me to approve such an absurd balance sheet. Whose balance sheet is this?"

The assistant replied, "It is the balance sheet of a mother's love, sir." The CA was speechless.

Bill further says in a stern voice, "Dear friends, do you want to know who that Chartered accountant was, who disapproved that balance sheet?"

The members are listening in rapt attention to Bill.

Bill continues, "Unfortunately we all. We are those Chartered accountants. We the professionals, the educated class, uxorious people, the smart people, the ones who have big houses, big cars, big jobs, the ones who pretend to be the good citizens. We all fall into this category. We never acknowledge the love of our mother, her care, her unconditional support. We never show any gratitude towards our mother. The sacrifices, the pains, the sufferings she had gone through, but never expressed and yet kept smiling. We just celebrate and speak well on such occasions, but after all what sentiments do we carry? How many members today have brought their mothers along to celebrate Mother's Day, I bet no one."

Bill pauses for a moment. There is complete silence in the audience.

Bill now lowers his voice and says, "However before I put my fingers on you, let me admit that first I am the culprit. I never gave any attention to my mother. My mother wanted to see me, but I was always busy in my work. When she came and stayed with me, I never had time to sit with her and talk even for a minute. Even at home I was always busy with my business. I am sorry to admit that the last time when she called me to visit her home, I was indeed busy with my Persian cat who was ill. I spend the weekend looking after my cat and on Monday I got the news that my mother passed away. I still remember she used to say, "You are always busy with your work and I am left all alone. After your father passed away, you are my only wealth."

Bill's voice begins to falter slightly but he continues by saying, "I did a grave mistake in my life and we all are doing, I suppose. We are more concerned about our pets than our parents. This is the new society, our new culture, our new way of living. We give much more time to pets than parents.

I have my deep regrets now but that cannot bring my mother back or the moment when she must have died, waiting to see my face. I feel so sorry. I have lost those beautiful eyes, always looking with tenderness and love, I have lost those beautiful and divine words that used to heal my wounds, I have lost my temple, my church, my everything."

Bill becomes wistful for a moment, takes a pause and continues in a low tone.

"Thanks friends. I am really sorry for being so blunt today. However, life has given me good lessons and I relinquish all my hypocrisies now."

Bill's speech is straight, unembellished and deeply poignant and he steps down from the stage.

Steve is amazed and so is the audience. There is a big round of applause for Bill.

Now it's Steve's turn. Steve is called upon the stage.

Steve has an incandescent personality which exhibits profound balance like an ascetic. He is tall, straight with a well-formed body. Steve is quite generous and calm but looks very energetic. There is a blaze of glory in his personality. His personality emanates an aura of culture, confidence and wisdom. He is fascinating and immediately catches the attention of the audience, as he steps on the stage.

Steve addresses the audience with most unfeigned respect and starts his speech.

"Dear friends,

I recall one of my experiences on this auspicious day. There was a time I was working in Bill's organization. It was long time ago. Bill wanted to recruit a good secretary for him. At that time the company was small. So, the criteria were not very stringent and hence the HR had arranged for a walk-in interview.

Lot of candidates came, experienced, inexperienced, male, female etc.

However, one girl who had just completed her graduation came for the interview. She was quite nervous. When I started the interview, she spoke very slowly. She gave her introduction in a suppressed tone and rambled sometimes. She was diffident in expressing her credentials. I could barely understand her. She was shy and feeling nervous.

She answered some of the questions but because of her trepidation she could not present herself explicitly and confidently.

After the interview I asked her, "From where did you get the reference of this job opening?"

She replied, "My mother found it. Generally, she reads the newspaper, especially the column of job openings. She identified this opportunity and asked me to come here."

"Were you interested to come?" I asked.

"Yes, I want the job, but I am feeling a bit nervous." She admitted.

I could understand that she was a normal girl basically from a typical middle-class background, who never had any job exposure in her life, and would obviously feel nervous. However, the girl's academic records were good, and I think what she needed was a small mental boost which could elevate her confidence and prepare her better.

Hence, I said, "It seems you are quite intelligent. Your mark sheet is fairly good. The way you have given the interview I am satisfied except for the little nervousness which I can understand, happens with most of the people on their first time. I see a lot of merits in you, and I think you are going to do great in your career."

The moment I uttered these few words of her appreciation, there was beatific smile on her face. First time she looked into my eyes.

I repeated, "Don't be anxious, whenever you go for the interview, go with all the confidence, don't bother about the job, be cool, remain calm and confident and lots of opportunities will follow you."

"So do I get this job," asked the girl curiously.

I replied, "I cannot assure you that. Basically, this opening is for my boss, Mr. Bill, who is a very enigmatic person, I don't know who he will select. But don't rate yourself with the upshot of this interview. Whether you get this job or not, it doesn't matter, since you have merits, you can get better jobs than this one. Just keep trying."

The girl was relaxed and seemed to feel better. Now she started expressing herself. She started speaking better. It seemed that she wanted to talk more with me. She began asking me questions, and one by one I provided all the answers. The conversation continued for further twenty minutes, her response improved, and she spoke more confidently.

Well, the interview was over. Unfortunately, the girl wasn't selected, but I suppose I was able to obliterate her fear and anxiety.

Some six to seven years later, I was just roaming in a shopping mall and all of a sudden, a voice came from behind. A smart looking girl with a lot of confidence stood in front of me asking, "Sir, do you remember me?"

I saw this girl, in her new looks and countenance and I could barely recognize her. I was unable to recall her. So, I said, "No" in a state of bewilderment.

She said, "I am Claire. I am the one who came for the interview couple of years ago. I was extremely nervous, and you boosted my confidence and put all the positive energy in me, do you recall?"

"Yes Claire, now I do," I replied with a smile.

She added, "After that interview I felt very confident. Though now I realize how poor my performance was, but still you ignored what reflected from my outside and you recognized my inner potential. Your words were, as if someone held my hand and gave me a huge thrust in my life. Your words gave a new meaning and a completely new stream of energy within me. It was a blessing. It was a transformational experience.

After that interview I started giving more interviews and finally I got selected in a good company. Today I am working for one of the best companies in the world. I am progressing by leaps and bounds. I always think of you and wanted to see you and personally thank you. Serendipitously I met you here."

Claire added, "It was because of you that my life took a turn. That day if I had not met you, probably I would have never reached this level. I attribute all my success to you."

I smiled and said, "I appreciate your feelings Claire, but let me correct you slightly. You know actually who is responsible for all your success?"

Claire asked surprisingly, "Who?"

I said, "It is your mother."

I further added, "The job opening was founded by your mother, it was she who compelled and motivated you to come for the interview, it is her blessings that everything went so well in your first interview, and then finally you got the job, where you deserved better and you became so successful in life. Frankly speaking, my part is hardly nothing in comparison to what your mother has done. My role is just like a guest appearance in your story. If you actually look, your complete success attributes to your mother."

Claire was once again surprised. She thought for a while, paused and said, "You are right Steve, I never thought of it that way. But yes, I agree with you, it was my mother who used to stay awake whole day and night to help me in my studies, she used to sleep late and get up early to wake me up for my exams, she used to look after the whole house, my father, my younger brother, we were not very rich, but she never complained and she practically gave everything of her, her time, her energy, her pleasures, her youth. Right from the beginning, the day I learned to walk, eat, speak, and write, she has always been with me. She is the ocean of love and compassion, who dedicated her whole life for us, never expected anything in return. She is my angel of love. Her soft arms, solicitous eyes, gentle and a warm hug are the real treasures of my life."

While Claire said this, her eyes were glistening with tears.

Claire said, "Steve you are indeed right. I have missed the bigger picture. Ofcourse I will be always grateful to you for what you have done for me, but today once again you have enlightened me about the most important part of my life i.e., my mother. I am enamored by your wisdom and incisive words. Thanks once again."

Steve adds further, "Friends, we generally fail to recognize the most important person in our life. The one who has contributed the most with her body, time and energy, our mother.

Mother's Day is not to bring chocolates or flowers for her, it's a day when you commit yourself to become something, so that the one who has brought you in this world, shall be proud of, it is a time when you commit yourself to return her the rewards she deserves, for the unconditional love she has showered upon you.

All the days like Father's Day, Mother's Day, Women's Day, Valentine's Day we celebrate, are not the days of celebration, they are the days when we commit ourselves to do something meaningful in our life, else celebration of these days is insignificant. Celebrating Mother's Day and then not having time for her, celebrating Women's Day and carrying gender inequality and disparity in heart, do you think that's appropriate? Celebrating Valentine's Day with roses, chocolates and gifts, but at the same time having no commitment in relationship, is all a meaningless affair.

Our celebrations are becoming more meaningless day by day. We are all getting towards pleasures, fun and enjoyment, whereas what is indeed required in this world is Commitment and Character.

Hence my friends, whatever day we are celebrating, kindly check if there is any commitment or else these celebrations will merely become a joke, just for fun. Unfortunately, this will debase our society and our future generation.

Let us commit ourselves to do something great, something more meaningful, something that makes sense in life, something that our new generation can learn, something that contributes value to our society, something that gives more meaning to our relationships, our family and our Character."

Steve takes a small pause and continues.

"I hope my message is simple and clear. It has been a pleasure being here. Thanks friends."

Steve completes his speech with warmth, passion and eloquence. The audience is transfixed with Steve's speech and there is a tumultuous applause once again.

The function is over. Bill and Steve together prepare to disembark. They are cheered by a lot of people. It seems, they have enraptured the audience.

Suddenly Bill and Steve come across an old lady, with a serene smile on her face, saying, "Thank you for such an invigorating and stupendous speech. You both are simply great. I am inexplicably thrilled. Bill you are like a Lion, and Steve you are like an angel. Your speeches have made indelible impression on everyone. God bless you both with good health and long life."

Bill fees very happy and very delighted.

Bill and Steve are back in their car.

Steve asks Bill, "You were quite bold and blunt today."

Bill says, "Steve I don't give two hoots to anything now. This club is a club for the rich class, all pretentious people like me. They don't give a shit to anything except money and power. I just came as matter of my duty, that's all. I am not an entertainer who would regale them with some stories or jokes or give some sanctimonious speech.

However, I feel good by blurting all the truth today. It has given me some respite from my guilts. I feel I have indeed earned something today."

"What's that?" asks Steve.

"The blessings of that lady," replies Bill.

Steve smiles and now there is silence in the car.

Steve is enjoying the ride. They are back home. It's time for lunch. They have their lunch and now Bill and Steve are once again in the library.

After some time Bill says, "Steve you were really good at taking interviews and selecting people. If I was Claire, I would have fallen in love with you."

Bill smiles and then laughs gently at Steve.

Steve replies, "I am a professional Bill. You know I never indulged in such acts."

Bill says, "I know Steve. You have always performed your duties conscientiously. I was just joking."

Bill takes a pause and then asks, "Steve, tell me what was your criteria to recruit people. All those people selected under your auspices were quite competent and also reliable. I was always keen to know what metrics did you use to analyze their skills. What exactly shall an interviewer look in a good candidate?"

Steve replies, "Before I answer your question Bill, let me tell you something. Generally, in an Interview, I have seen most of the Interviewers they try to discommode the interviewee. They take interviews as an opportunity to prove that they know better rather than trying to know the candidate precisely. They regiment every aspect of the Interview, making the candidate more nervous and the environment totally unconducive. Basically, the term Interview means, Inter and view, which means seeing each other. Interview is to assess a candidate's credentials, his skills and check his suitability for the job. You can also assess his weaknesses, but most of the Interviewers after learning about the candidate's weaknesses, try to demean them. You can smell ego in their questions and in their tone. They will ask questions based on the subject, which they are good at and not the candidate. I generally ask the candidate, on those subjects, in which he/she is confident and comfortable. Instead of checking their general knowledge which most of the companies do, I check their depth in their specialized field. That gives me an indication of how sincere, thorough and hardworking they are and can be.

However, even if they do not qualify to my standards or my criteria, I don't demean them. I never demotivate anyone in my life. Whatever skills people have, or they don't have, everyone still deserves respect. We have no right to judge and disparage anyone, just because they do not satisfy our requirements pertinently.

As Albert Einstein said, "Everybody is a genius. But if you judge a fish by its ability to climb a tree, it will live its whole life believing, that it is stupid."

Bill, I have an intelligent quotient (IQ) of 125, a fact that alludes to me being almost a genius, but there is a huge disparity in my skill set. When I want to alter some settings in my mobile phone, I can't do it easily. I become dull. Hence, let's not judge people with our perspective only.

Further my philosophy is different. I cannot give job to everyone, but I can atleast motivate and prepare them better for the next opportunity. That's exactly what I did with Claire. I always close my interview sessions with a positive note to the candidate and wishing them good luck in their future endeavors."

Bill replies, "Absolutely right Steve. I hope this world could learn from you."

Bill further asks, "Well Steve, can you please let me know what are those basic qualities that you see specifically in a candidate."

Steve replies, "Bill there are five basic qualities that determine whether the selected candidate will be worthy or not. These five basic qualities are:

1. Attitude.
2. Intelligence.
3. Enthusiasm.
4. Integrity.
5. Interpersonal skills.

Bad attitude is a disease, the more it permeates in your mind, the more ignorant you become about it. Just like alcohol, after some time you suffer from oblivion and you are totally unaware of your self being. Next day you won't remember what you have done or passed through. Bad attitude does not permit you to realize your flaws and idiosyncrasies. You become irrational in your behavior.

If people's attitude is not good, then they are good for nothing. Without a good attitude, they will be totally disengaged in their team, their colleagues will start avoiding them and finally they will make the complete environment unconducive. Inspite of being in the system, they will be out of the system, just like oil in water. Unfortunately, it is a chronic disease making a person incorrigible.

Secondly without intelligence, people saturate after a certain level. Intelligence is the foundation. It's a God's gift. Through intelligence, human being possesses the cognitive abilities like to learn, understand, develop skills, apply logic, enhance creativity, conceptualize, conceive, reason, make decisions, resolve problems, make plans, communicate, perform, differentiate between the right and the wrong, make relations, and finally grow. Intelligence is the CPU and if the CPU is poor, the complete system will be dull.

Thirdly without enthusiasm our intelligence will rot after some time, just like an Iron sword lying in open, which will corrode very soon and will be good for nothing. Now a days people are quite pompous, carrying a high opinion about their capabilities, but when it comes to hard work, they have no zeal, they shirk from their responsibilities and work. They are indolent and languid. I call them mentally impotent."

Bill interrupts and says, "You are right Steve. I experienced the same thing with a lot of people. Infact people despite being competent or with excellent academic record, do not have the zeal to work. I don't understand where does their enthusiasm go."

Steve replies, "Bill all enthusiasm goes away in multitudinous distractions. In one of my books of quotes, I have stated.

"The way people are knowledgeable today they were never before, unfortunately the way people are distracted today; they were never before."

This is the present condition of people today. Distraction is taking all their energy and they become mentally impotent. Hence one should remain focussed in life, in order to spare his energy in the right way.

Coming to the fourth quality which is Integrity, without which, all attitude, intelligence and enthusiasm will be a total waste, leading to finally failure in life. People without integrity can be engaged in treason, embezzlement, malfeasance in office, bribery or larceny, or connive at crimes involving moral turpitude. Basically, all skills that they are gifted, will contaminate and become a curse in their life. Eventually it will debase their character and ultimately life will be full of regrets and shame.

Further Interpersonal skills, the fifth quality, are quite important. If you intend to have a cohesive team, you need to have good interpersonal skills.

I would like to put it this way.

"In your academic career your hard work is important to succeed, whereas in your professional career teamwork is important to succeed."

In professional career you cannot succeed without a good team. That is why most of the highly educated people fail in their jobs, inspite of their technical or management knowledge, as they lack good Interpersonal skills. To have good Interpersonal skills, you need to have good understanding, humility, you should listen first and then speak, a good moral character because that is what people notice first in you before they follow you, treating everyone with equality, having compassion for people and finally having the ability to become a role model. This all will improve the camaraderie.

As the U.S. President, Theodore Roosevelt said,

"People don't care how much you know until they know how much you care."

People, who do not have the ability to work in a team because of their poor Interpersonal skills, will not succeed beyond a certain limit. Without Interpersonal skills, relationships will become sterile. Such people cannot be given higher positions in any organization.

The above five qualities are common in all successful people, Bill. I only see the basic five qualities."

Bill asks, "What about knowledge?"

Steve replies, "That is my last consideration. If you are looking people for a long-term relationship, knowledge does not matter so much. People who have these basic five skills, acquiring knowledge is not a big deal for them."

Bill further asks, "Steve I want to know how to control people. I understand that recruiting the best talent is one thing, but then how to control these people?"

Steve replies, "Don't try to control people Bill. They are not slaves. Basically, people can never be controlled, they can only be conditioned to the best of their abilities.

The difference between your management and my management style was that you controlled people with your power and authority, but I used to condition them with my leadership qualities. Controlling is momentary, till the time you have the power and authority, you can control them, but the moment you lose your authority you lose control.

Conditioning is a long-term process. It transforms people from Iron to Gold. However, it takes merits to condition people. It does not happen overnight. It happens only with leadership qualities.

People who are conditioned, don't require any external agency to control them. They are like the candles which have started giving light. Just give them a good environment and they will perform to the best of their abilities and potential.

Good leaders condition their people, good parents condition their children, good teachers condition their students, only tyrants control their people. However, once they lose their power, everything goes haywire.

Bill, you managed people by being coercive and I managed people being cohesive and that's why sometimes you were like a Step boss.

Bill interrupts and says in a quizzical tone, "Step Boss Steve, what is this term Step Boss!!!"

Steve replies, "Bill, when a Boss is concerned only towards his selfish desires and ignores the priorities of his employees, he becomes a step boss, like a stepfather, a stepbrother or stepmother. The corporate world is full of such step bosses. Don't be surprised."

Bill chuckles and says, "Step Boss! What kind of definition is this?"

"What kind of attitude people have," Steve smiles and replies.

Bill says, "OK Steve, I cannot argue with you. What you are saying is probably right. I understand we put a lot of pressure on employees and the only target of any organization is to get more and more, more from the employees, more from the clients, more from machines, more from everything, irrespective of the ramifications. But I have seen even employees are embroiled with greed. They want more & more, more salaries, foreign tours, luxury cars, lavish life, bigger houses, expensive gadgets, extravagant holiday trips etc. All this comes from money, all money comes from profits and all profits comes from sales. There is no other option. Moreover, people want to succeed overnight, so we give them exactly in commensurate to their aspirations. What's wrong in that. It's not that we are taking advantage, but it is their aspirations also, which are greedy and impatient. So, I think, it's a perfect match.

Moreover Steve, we are running a business for pecuniary benefits and not engaged in some eleemosynary work."

Steve says, "I agree with you Bill. People are deluded with cupidity. Everyone is in rush to catch this Royal train of their career, with all the extravagance and a pompous life, in which all the best material of the world exists, except for a good health and a peaceful mind. Moreover, the train is moving so fast, that we cannot see all that is so valuable and meaningful, lying outside.

We come out only when we lose our capacity to keep pace with this fast-moving train. However, by the time people realize, it is too late, they come to an irreversible deplorable situation."

Bill takes a small breath, and it seems he is tired. He wants to take a small break.

He asks Steve, "Steve, in the evening I am supposed to go to my relative's wedding. I have to leave within an hour. I would be grateful if you can accompany me."

Steve is not so keen, but Bill insists and Steve cannot avoid his appeal.

Bill asks Steve to take some rest, but Steve wants to be in the library, read some books, have his favorite Columbian coffee and probably stroll in the garden.

Bill goes to his room to take some rest.

After one hour Bill is ready, they start for the wedding reception. The venue is on the countryside. Bill and Steve are finally there.

It's a normal marriage reception. The bridegroom singing songs, dancing and being cheered by everyone. Some youngsters and newly wedded couples, join the dance with the bridegroom, making the event more joyful.

At one corner there is a bar. Most of the gathering is around the bar. People are enjoying their drinks. Some are enjoying their cocktails. Some seemed inebriated and entertaining themselves with lousy jokes.

The food is delectable. The atmosphere is very convivial.

However, it is a good chance for Bill and Steve to catch up with their old friends and relatives. It is quite a happy event. The groom is the son of Bill's cousin. Bill meets his cousin, and he takes him to one corner and gives him something, surreptitiously. His cousin seems to be quite obliged. However, both seem to be happy.

Bill is quite tired and finally they are now on their way, back home.

In the car Steve asks Bill, "What did you give to your cousin, while taking him to the corner."

Bill says, "I gave him a cheque of fifty thousand dollars."

Bill added, "My cousin is not a rich man. They are a middle-class family. The expense of this marriage must be a big burden to them. He is like my real brother. So, I gave them this money, just as a help."

Steve says, "Bill, I want to ask you something. In the morning you asserted when I gave ten dollars to that beggar, that in case if the beggar misused the money, like if he drinks alcohol, I will be held accountable for his actions. Right now, you gave fifty thousand dollars to your brother, for the expense of this marriage. They are already serving alcohol in this party. A big part of your money is being spent for alcohol. If I will be held accountable for ten dollars, what will happen to you, for giving fifty thousand dollars. Your penalty will be five thousand times more than mine.

Bill is totally appalled and speechless and he gazes at Steve reprovingly.

Steve says, "Bill you see the flaws of poor people, but why can't you see the flaws of your brother. While giving to a beggar you analyze hundred times, while giving to your relatives or to your business friends, you don't think for a second."

Steve continues, "Bill you know all the rich people of this city. You have been dealing with them so closely. Tell me who are bigger culprits, the beggar on the streets or your rich friends? Who do you think are involved more into illicit activities?"

Bill replies, "Obviously the rich people."

Steve says, "On one side we have these needy people so called beggars and on the other side we have these greedy people, so called the rich class. While giving one or two dollars to the poor people we think hundred times, but on the other hand, while giving to the rich class there are no such moral rules."

"Are you pointing towards me Steve?" asks Bill in an icy tone.

"No Bill don't take it personally. I am talking dispassionately. I just want you to open your eyes and look on both the sides neutrally. Don't become biased." replies Steve.

Steve continues, "Unfortunately power and money hides all the flaws and idiosyncrasies of the rich people. But the poor fails, and he remains exposed."

Steve asks further, "Bill tell me one thing, while giving bribe of millions, did you ever think the way you have been reasoning while giving ten dollars to a beggar."

Bill smiles and replies, "Never Steve."

Steve says, "Bill, just analyze your reasoning level. On one hand you are so apprehensive and on the other you are so carefree. This is just like having elephantitis in one leg and polio in the other. A total imbalance and disparity in your thinking attitude."

Bill laughs and says, "Good Steve. Very good clarification. This is what I like about you. Though you put me into a tight corner, but I appreciate the way you put things so sensibly and logically."

Steve is now silent and Bill too. After five minutes it seems some confusion has erupted in Bill's mind.

Bill unbale to control, asks Steve, "Steve there is still one confusion, which remains in my mind. I would like to hark back to the same topic where we started."

"What's that Bill?" asks Steve.

Bill asks, "Steve tell me one thing. When you give some money to a beggar and let's say if he misuses it in an illicit act, are we accountable for his actions. What is the fact. I really want to know the correct answer."

Steve replies, "Bill I used to think exactly the way you do and so does the whole world. However, after learning all the wisdom of the world, I got the correct answer.

Well Bill, it never happens the way we think or the whole world believes. When you give something to someone there are two things which are important. They are:

1. Intention.
2. Awareness.

God sees your intentions first and then your actions. If your intentions are impure, it does not matter if your actions are good, it will be taken into bad accounts. For e.g., if you are helping a young girl in your office, your actions seem to be good, but behind your refined manners and artificial elegance, lies your treacherous intentions to have an extra marital affair and use the girl for your lust, hence such good-looking actions will be considered as sin.

Hence foremost your intentions should be pure.

Secondly whatever you do in your life, do it with awareness which means apply all your moral intellect and a rational reasoning, taking into account the consequences of your act and the vision of the future, keeping in view the welfare of the society, keeping the same spirit for every human being whether they are known or unknown to you, without any discrimination, and finally the most important is, keeping God in witness.

Any action, done with good intentions and awareness, will always reap good fruits. However, it does not matter what happens thereafter, you will not be considered responsible for it.

Nature sees your intentions and your awareness. If both are justified at that moment, that act will always be taken into good books and be rewarded.

Now let's say if you gave some money to a beggar with an intention to help him. Moreover, the beggar seems to be needy, as per your awareness. Now since your intentions and your awareness is justified, your deed will be taken into good books. However, if that beggar uses that money immorally, which is beyond your knowledge, then that beggar will be held accountable for his misdeeds not you. As far as you are considered, you will always reap good rewards.

Hence Bill before doing anything keep your intentions pure and perform your acts with Awareness.

Awareness is the fundamental basis of human life. "**Awareness is above truth**."

Bill looks quizzically at Steve and asks, "Steve your answer seems to be quite logical and correct. I completely agree to what you say. However, I am once again confused as you said that "Awareness is above truth." How can this be possible. Truth is the basis of life, fundamental requirement of morality. Truth is everything. How can awareness be above truth. This seems to be quite confusing."

Steve replies, "Bill, it's too late now. We would be reaching home very soon. I shall share a small wondrous story with you tomorrow morning and I hope I would be able to clarify your confusion."

Bill replies, "Fine Steve. I would be eager to listen to the story."

Finally, Bill and Steve reach home.

Chapter 4

THE ONLY THING WHICH IS DISINTEGRATED WITH THE UNIVERSE

Steve as usual gets up early and goes to the garden.

The sun has just risen, a shining beautiful globe with its golden light, just about to shower life on the whole planet. The birds are chirping and the breeze is still cool, with a vivifying atmosphere. It is wonderful to see the dew drops on the leaves of the plants. In the entire day, this particular moment, which is the purest form of nature, isolated from the worldly noise and activities, filled with serene silence, seems to have some spiritual essence. There is some magic, as if the whole creation is meditating. The whole world seems like an Ashram, as if God is making himself evident in everything and promising a new beginning for everyone. As if nature has once again reached its youth and energizing the whole planet, with its abundance. Each and every life form, integrating itself as one with Earth, Energy and Time. Nothing is more pleasant or spiritual in the entire Universe, than these moments during the dawn. The experience of these moments is ineffable.

Steve just sits, relaxes and energizes himself into these magical moments. It seems like he is meditating, not alone, but with the whole creation. Steve seems to be integrating himself more and more with Nature and the Universe. His entire mind, body and soul, seems to be transfigured by the magical moments of the morning.

After one hour of relaxing and strolling in the garden, Steve is back in his room and now getting ready for the breakfast.

As usual Steve and Bill have their breakfast and finally back in the library.

Bill seems to be quite keen to listen to the story on Awareness. He insists Steve to share the enlightening story.

Steve starts by saying, "Once there was a man, who was in search of a Guru. He had one condition, that he would perceive that person as his Guru, who has never spoken any lies, not a single word, in his entire life. According to that man, such a Guru would be worthy of his veneration.

So, one day that man set forth in his search. He wandered all over the world but could not find a Guru, who hasn't lied.

While returning back home in total dismay and despair, he met an ascetic on his way. He shared his desire with the ascetic that he has been in search of a Guru who has never spoken any lies in his entire life. He also expressed his disappointment as he could not find anyone in this world. The ascetic laughed on him and said "It was totally unnecessary for you to wander all over the world. There is a saint just outside this village, living in the woods. Just go to him and your fervent desire for such a Guru will be fulfilled."

The man got overly excited and joyously started his journey with zest.

He reached the place before dusk and under one tree he saw a saint garbed in a white loincloth, seated in a lotus posture and his face suffused with divine light. The man just at the sight of the saint, was mesmerized.

Before the man could express his desire, the saint said, "I know you are in search of a Guru who has never spoken a lie, in his entire life. You are valiantly seeking for such a man to be your Guru. Don't worry, you will not go bare handed from this place."

The man was surprised with his clairvoyance. He bowed down and touched his sacred feet.

The saint further instructed the man, "From tomorrow you can come here, spend a few days with me and I hope your purpose shall be served."

The man started going to the saint and would spend few hours with him. They would have discourses, the man learned meditation and other important aspects of life. The experience was quite enlightening.

One day while the saint was preaching, all of a sudden, a girl came rushing towards the saint, trembling all over with fear.

She whimpered, "Please help me, there are some miscreants after me, they are trying to molest me. Please save me."

The saint immediately responded and said, "Don't worry. Nothing will happen to you. Just go behind the tree. There is a small cave, hide yourself over there. No one will be able to find you there."

The girl immediately rushed towards the cave and hid herself.

Within two minutes the miscreants came and asked the Guru in a strident voice, "Have you seen a young girl anywhere around here?"

The saint replied valiantly, "No one has ever been here since morning."

The miscreant replied, "But we have seen one girl rushing towards this side."

The saint once again retorted, "She might have come towards this side, but I suppose she might have gone to that direction towards the village. On that side there is a road approaching the village and the only possibility I see, is the girl running in that direction."

The miscreants believed the saint and brusquely departed towards the village road, which was exactly in the opposite direction where the girl was hiding.

Once the miscreants left, the girl came out.

She thanked the saint and explained, "We are tourist, I was here with my family and I was scampering in the woods with my siblings. Unfortunately, I got lost and came across these miscreants. They were all drunk and one of them tried to physically assault me. I understood their nefarious intentions and somehow I managed to escape and started running. With no clue of any direction, I came here and saw both of you. I think you have been manifested by God to help me. Thank you so much."

The saint asked one of his followers to go along with the girl and leave her safely to her family.

However, on seeing all this that man was very much disconcerted. The saint whom he worshipped and considered as a man who never spoke any lies in his entire life, was witnessed speaking utter lies to the miscreants. The man was totally perturbed and stared at the Guru in consternation.

Before the man could say anything, the saint realized the disturbance, going in this man's mind.

The saint bluntly asked, "Are you disappointed with my lies?"

The man replied impertinently, "Ofcourse. This is what I didn't expect from you. How come you speak lies like this."

The saint said, "Come here my boy. Listen to me carefully."

The saint spoke placatingly, "Had I not spoken the lies, my truth would have exacerbated the situation. The girl would have been raped and probably got killed. Just imagine the suffering that girl might have to undergo. Secondly just try to imagine, how her parents would have felt, after knowing the harrowing details of this incident. I am surprised that my lie has disconcerted you, but you do not seem to be worried about the atrocities which could have brutalized the girl, if I had spoken the truth. How can you ignore the consequences blithely, this would be extremely callous."

The man was deeply mortified.

The saint now asks, "Let's say, if this happened to your own daughter, how would you feel? Reply to me?"

The man was completely bewildered and said sheepishly, "It would tear me apart and would be more painful than my own death."

The saint continues, "Exactly. I think now you are getting the point. So let me share with you the ultimate lesson and clear your obscurity about truth.

"AWARENESS IS ABOVE TRUTH"

Truth without awareness can be mere stupidity, it can be meaningless, it can be poisonous, it can be a more ugly and dirty than a lie, it can be painful to others, it can be callous, it can be preposterous, it can blind you and the most important thing it can be immoral. It is awareness that discerns the morality in truth. If truth is not reinforced with Awareness, it is futile.

Let me tell you boy, even if these miscreants would have taken my life, I would have never told the truth. Although I spoke a lie, but still, it is above truth.

A small child does not speak any lies. If you are looking for a human being who has never spoken a lie, then better go and follow small children. However, they cannot enlighten you.

The basic difference between the whole creation and human being is just Awareness. Lion may be the king of jungle, Dinosaurs may have been the largest creatures on earth, a Cheetah may be the fastest animal on earth, but still we human beings are considered to be the best creation of God. This is just because of one thing i.e., "Awareness."

This is the most precious gift given by God to us. Awareness is the basis of humanity and not truth. Awareness is the ultimate stage towards liberation. The more the Awareness, the more will be humanity in a human being or else we shall all become like animals just eat, sleep, enjoy, reproduce and die one day turning into dust.

Unfortunately, we are all so badly entangled in this superstitious world, with our own fallacies, that we have lost every clue of the right direction. Without awareness, people are becoming blind with open eyes, sleeping, though the body is awake and finally dead in a living body. Hence elevate yourself, see things beyond the veil of your confused intellect, your obscured understanding and a distorted belief system and you will find wisdom and ultimate liberation.

The man now realized the ultimate truth. He felt entreatingly at the saint's feet and said, "In the last few days I thought I am very wise. My fallacy empowered my ego and made me blind, but today after this enlightening experience, I have realized how foolish and ignorant I was. You have blessed me with the wisdom, which has dispelled my darkness and destroyed my delusion about truth. Your enlightening words have enlarged and vivified my perception towards truth. I am deeply thankful to you for this grace and epiphany."

The story ends here.

Bill responds, "Great story Steve. Very clear and enlightening. Steve, these are small little things in life which confuses us badly. Such a complex theory about truth and awareness, a common man could never comprehend. However, such a simple story, has made the meaning so clear. Steve, you speak so eloquently and the way you represent the convoluted subjects so simply, I am surprised. Thanks Steve. I appreciate your wisdom and clarity on the subjects."

Steve says, "Fine Bill, I think it's time for some coffee. Don't you think?"

"Ofcourse Steve, but with those handmade biscuits from Belgium," replies Bill.

Bill smiles, lifts the phone and orders for the coffee and the biscuits.

Steve and Bill continue their conversation during their coffee. After the coffee Bill has some more important questions to ask.

Bill asks Steve, "Steve I have some basic questions about life. I would be grateful if you can enlighten me."

Steve says, "Tell me Bill."

Bill asks, "Why all this creation, why this Universe, why this life? What is the purpose of all this creation? Why are we here, what is the purpose of human life? Why human being is the most unhappy creature on earth, the most insane species and making life miserable for self and everyone? Why the best creation of God is the worst performer in the world, Why Steve, why?"

Steve replies, "Bill all this is not that easy to understand. The questions that you have asked are of great wisdom. Unfortunately, such questions arise only once you have realized the worthlessness of this materialistic world. Before this realization we are all entangled into a monotonous life, monotonous means, a life which is based only on two basic activities i.e., surviving (eat, drink, sleep and seek security) and seeking pleasure (physical and mental). Each and every human being in this world is entangled into these two basic activities. Unfortunately, it is an endless affair, leading nowhere and resulting into an interminable struggle. However, the question regarding the existence of this creation and ourselves, comes only when someone realizes that life is like a dream. A dream which is extremely fragile, which can collapse anytime and once the dream collapses, you have nothing with you. So is this life, once encountered with death, we leave everything behind, including our body, our family, all our belongings, etc. no matter how important it was to us, while we lived.

You already had this realization, Bill. Am I correct?"

Bill replies, "Absolutely Steve."

Steve continues, "So Bill your question has come with a deep realization. It can be answered in various ways, but it won't be appropriate. The precise reply comes only from the spiritual perspective and not just from the scientific aspect. Bill in order to answer all your questions I will start from the beginning, from the point this evolution started. Till the time we don't understand the basics of evolution, it will be difficult to comprehend any further details."

Bill says, "Interesting Steve please continue, I am keen to listen."

Steve continues, "There are various theories about evolution Bill. The whole subject seems a bit too arcane for the common man. How did it happen, when did it happen, who made it happen and the most important question is why it happened. I will reply to all the questions one by one and lastly your question why the best creation of God i.e., human being is the worst performer in the world and in the most miserable condition.

However, let us start with the basic question about this creation i.e. How and when did it happen?

How and when did it happen?

The most accepted theory about evolution is the big bang theory, developed in 1927. The big bang event is the single event, which was the genesis of all matter and life in the Universe. This theory was further developed in the following years and is considered to be the most credible scientific explanation of how the Universe was created. The theory gives details about the origins of the universe from its early formations to its modern-day evolutions. However, more interesting is to know what was there before the big bang? I would like to start from the point which is before the big bang. What was there in this Universe before the big bang? Bill as I told you the answer will remain incomplete if I look at the scientific reference only, hence those gaps and empty spaces where science couldn't reach, I have taken references from the spiritual science, not blindly but very rationally.

It is believed that before the big bang there was nothing except extremely dense cloud. This cloud was incomprehensible. It was matter or non-matter, no one can ever define. The cloud was massive. The cloud seemed to be reinforced with spirit. This spirit was the intelligence and the energy holding it. At this moment there was no existence of time. It was a Universe integrated into itself. Nothing appeared to be different or changing. It was immutable. There was total darkness, there was no earth, no sky, no air, no water, there was no day or night, no moon or sun, no existence of time, no life, no death, there was complete stillness. Just like a saint in a primal, profound meditative absorption, an absolute silence and tranquility.

Then there was a one-word command from the spirit. Most of the religions state that the evolution started with one word. With the incantation of this word, the big bang happened. Most people think of the big bang as a big explosion. There are many misconceptions surrounding the big bang theory. For example, we tend to imagine a giant explosion, like a bomb going off. However, there was no explosion; there was a rapid expansion, an evolution. An explosion results into disintegration, leading to destruction, but evolution results into expansion, having everything integrated with each other. Just as a seed getting evolved into many different forms like the trunk, branches, leaves, flowers, fruits and finally making a complete tree, so was this evolution. The evolution of the seed into a tree, is not an explosion. The Universe evolved with all its energy, integrating the whole creation as one.

Spiritually if you see the whole universe is a one spreadsheet. If the whole universe was a different fragment, then very easily one galaxy which is moving with tremendous speed, would collide with another. This would keep on going endlessly. But this hardly happens, mainly because the whole universe is woven with one single chord which keeps everything under control, in a highly organized manner, complementing each other.

Bill, I will give you a small example. A small leaf of a grass, so small and having negligible weight, is also connected with the huge, gigantic Sun, which is around 148 million kilometers away from Earth. Without sunlight the grass would thin out and die. Though everything seems to be so huge, so far and disconnected, but the beauty of the creation is that despite all its diversities, it actually is interwoven and inexplicably one, complementing each other.

So, with the big bang the spirit transmuted its energy and intelligence into infinite forms. The cycle of time was initiated, and time came into existence.

Just one word and the series of complex reactions started. The evolution underwent a rapid and colossal expansion. Initially it evolved into matter, but all this formation was integrated with gravity. The forms and shapes are results of gravity and the intelligence, all set up into the space, which means billions of galaxies, planets, stars, suns etc. were formed from the ultimate cloud. The whole creation which came into existence, is unfathomable.

Time, gravity and matter, all three were reinforced with Intelligence. The common man overlooks the intelligence with which the Universe has been created, but the science is very much aware of this fact.

Once the matter was formed i.e., billions of galaxies, planets, stars, suns, then life came into existence. Right now, we are aware of life existing only on earth. So, on earth initially there were micro-organisms like bacteria, fungi which further developed into plants. There was tremendous complex mechanism which was followed to manifest life. Bill it is impossible to encapsulate the whole multifarious process of creation into words, but still, I am putting everything in a simple perspicuous manner, for our basic understanding. The first life seen in this universe was in plants. Then came reptiles, mammals, small insects and fishes. Fish was the first species having a bone in its body, thereafter, came the birds and other animals. As per science we human beings have actually evolved from fish.

Evolution diversified itself into various species. Science estimates that there must be trillions of species uptill now, out of which millions have extinct. We have been able to discover only a few. How this diversification happened, there are lot of assumptions, but there is no concrete evidence available to this theory, so far. This is how life and we human beings emerged, starting from the inception of this Universe, which gives a small indication but not the complete details.

Well coming to the next question when did this happen. As per the big bang theory, it is estimated that the evolution happened 13.7 billion years ago. As far as human beings are concerned our ancestors have been there for about six million years ago and the modern form of humans evolved about 200,000 years ago. Bill if we scale down the total time since the Universe evolved into 24 hours, then human beings have evolved only two seconds ago."

Steve says, "I hope I am clear upto this point Bill."

Bill says, "Very clear Steve, please continue."

As Steve starts there is call for lunch. The discussion is adjourned. Though Bill seems to be very keen to continue listening, but Steve does not have a choice. Steve and Bill both move on to the dining room.

After one hour they are back. They once again reassemble at the library.

Generally, Steve expects Bill to be slightly sluggish after the lunch, but Bill seems to be very enthusiastic to listen to Steve. The moment they sit, Bill asks, "Steve please continue with your topic. I am desperate to listen further."

Steve says, "OK Bill. So, when human beings came into existence, then came a perplexing question. The Question was:

"Who am I?"

This question came from an awakened human mind. Human being is the only species who is self-aware to a greater depth.

For instance, most of the animals are not aware about their existence. For e.g., animals can identify their hunger, their instincts, the world existing externally, but they fail to identify themselves. Lot of experiments have been conducted by putting various animals and birds in front of the mirror to check whether they can identify themselves or not. However, most of the species mistook their image as their enemy or someone else. They could not recognize that it was their own image.

The mirror test sometimes called the mark test, mirror self-recognition (MSR) test, is a behavioral technique developed in 1970 by American psychologist Gordon Gallup Jr. as an attempt to determine whether an animal possesses the ability of visual self-recognition. The MSR test is the traditional method for attempting to measure self-awareness.

In the classic MSR test, an animal is anesthetized and then marked (e.g., painted or a sticker attached) on an area of the body which the animal cannot normally see. When the animal regains its consciousness, it is given access to a mirror. If the animal then touches or investigates the mark, it is taken as an indication that the animal perceives the reflected image as an image of itself, rather than of another animal.

Yet most living species on the planet do not possess it. Out of hundreds of animals tested so far, only few animals have been proven to have any measurable degree of self-awareness. These are Orangutans, Chimpanzees, Gorillas, Bottlenose, Dolphins, Elephants and a few more.

Gordon Gallup, Jr., further experimentally investigated the possibility of self-recognition with two male and two female wild preadolescents chimpanzees, none of which had presumably seen a mirror previously. A multitude of behaviors were recorded upon introducing the mirrors to the chimpanzees. Initially, the chimpanzees made threatening gestures at their own images, ostensibly seeing their own reflections as threatening. Eventually, the chimps used their own reflections for self-directed responding behaviors, such as grooming parts of their body previously not observed without a mirror, picking their noses, making faces, and blowing bubbles at their own reflections.

Further the mirror test was performed by Mr. Helmut Prior and his colleagues, on the Eurasian magpie. The magpie is the first non-mammal to have been found to pass the mirror test. In 2008, the researchers applied a small red, yellow, blue & black sticker to the throat of five Eurasian magpies. The birds were then placed against a mirror. However, when the birds with colored stickers glimpsed themselves in the mirror, they tried to remove the sticker at their throats—a clear indication that they recognized the image in the mirror, as their own.

Further Amsterdam, Beulah (1972) performed the mirror self-recognition test (MSR) on infants. The experiment consisted in about 88 infants between 3 and 24 months old. In case of infants, between the age of 6 and 12 months, it was seen that a child typically sees a "sociable playmate" in the mirror and gave friendly gestures, reacting joyfully. From 12 to 18 months, the infants act embarrassed, shy, or fearful, sometimes puzzled in front of the mirror. Finally, at 18 months, few children recognize the reflection in the mirror as their own and by 20 to 24 months, self-recognition starts.

However, Bill, self-awareness is still limited in most of the human beings i.e., they recognize themselves the way the world has identified them. You can just go and ask this question to various people, that who they are, most of them will reply by telling their name, some will also add their professional designation like a manager or a general manager or the CEO or probably a president or the personal roles they are performing in their family like a father, husband, wife, mother, brother etc. Mostly people identify themselves with their qualifications, their nationality, caste, parent's name and some may like to boast about themselves with their achievements. We all have deluded ourselves with false identities.

But when all these names, designations, achievements fail and people realize the fragility of these identities, then this question "**Who am I**" arises with the right perspective and in the most meaningful way, the way it has now emerged from you. I don't think I need to explain more on this topic Bill. You have already experienced this."

"Yes Steve," replies Bill.

Steve continues.

"Bill, at this stage the person knows, I am not some name given by my parents or by the society, I am not the one as I perceive myself by the color of my skin, I am not the one the mirror shows to me every day, I am not the one who has qualified himself as some doctor, engineer, lawyer, a businessman, a singer, I am not the way science has defined me i.e. only body, I am not the one the society claims about me, I am not someone my friends, my relatives or the world has made their opinion or perceive about me, but I am indeed something more significant in this world. I am much more than what I have been given to understand, by the world.

This is true self-awareness where a person seeks the ultimate truth about his own-self and his existence in this mortal world."

Bill interrupts and asks eagerly, "So Steve who are we?"

Steve replies, "Bill I will answer to your question later, let me first complete one more point, i.e. Who is the Creator of all?"

Steve continues, "So Bill if you go to a theist and ask him about the Creator of this Universe, he would simply say, it is God. But instead of taking reference from a theist and concluding this matter so easily, let me analyze this matter more rationally and analytically.

Bill if you go to a scientist and ask him about the Creator, he will not have any precise answer, because he does not have any evidence. But a scientist who has gone deeper into the roots of creation, even in the absence of evidence, would accept the existence of some supreme intelligence, responsible for everything that exists.

The scientists know very well that everything happening in the universe is not by chance, but it is a well-organized phenomenon, happening on a massive scale, very precisely and very methodically. But due to lack of evidence and or we can say due to the limitations of science, which has constrained it to reach to the evidence, science cannot assert to conclude anything authentically in this matter.

Bill the problem with science is that it believes only in those things which can be seen, measured directly or indirectly by their scientific devices. For e.g., we cannot see air, but it can be felt through scientific instruments, hence it is acceptable to science. We cannot feel the atmospheric pressure of one bar around us, but the scientific instruments can measure it. We cannot define the proportion of Nitrogen, Oxygen, Carbon dioxide and other gases in Air, whereas science can do so with its scientific instruments. Hence science believes only in those things, which can be seen or made evident directly or indirectly through its scientific instruments or experiments. Rest all is absent for science.

Sharing one more example that we studied in our school. As per science, work done is equal to force multiplied by physical displacement. If the physical displacement is zero work done will be zero.

Now as per this equation all scientists, doctors, engineers or I would say all professionals, since they are working with their intellect and no physical displacement is involved, they are doing absolutely no work. Hence, as per this equation work done is zero, which is incorrect. Basically, my point is not that the equation is wrong but what I mean to say is, that the theory of science does have its limitations. Science is unable to measure or evaluate any work done by our intellect. Similarly, science does not have any means to identify our mind, our soul, the supreme energy or the God. They have no equations; they have no instruments or equipment. Unfortunately, we believe what science states and we deny what science denies, without understanding the limitations of science.

Hence science despite of being aware of the tremendous intelligence pervading in the whole Universe, fail to recognize it, since it is beyond the capacity of their measuring instruments or their scientific equations.

Bill let me ask you one question.

Is there anything in your life which you have been using in your daily life, created on its own like a toothbrush, a stapler pin, some papers, a small pen or a pencil etc.?"

Bill thinks for a while and answers, "No Steve nothing."

Steve says, "So, Bill then how is it possible that such a huge infinite, unfathomable Universe is created on its own. Do you think such a colossal Creation is manifested on its own?

Bill let me give you a small example. Instead of telling you what profound miracles are going in our cosmos, I would like to have your attention to the fabulous miracles happening within our human life."

Steve asks, "Bill, do you believe that human brain is the most intelligent part of human body or the most knowledgeable gadget on earth?"

"Absolutely Steve, it's an undeniable truth. Brain is the quintessence of intelligence; do you have any doubts on this?" replies Bill.

Steve says, "OK Bill, before I conclude anything I would like to share something very spectacular.

Just pay attention to the sperm and the egg of the human beings, which are of microscopic size. During fertilization they combine together and become one cell, which is billion times smaller than our brain. Such a miniscule cell, which is invisible by the naked eye, makes the complete human body within nine months, whereas today with a population of seven billion people (which means seven billion brains) on this planet, and so exceedingly advanced technology and instruments, we have not been able to make even a small hair of human body. Forget about the hair, we have not been able to make a single drop of human blood.

Bill are you aware of the complex process going during the conception of human life. This one cell divides into many, which is called differentiation. During this process the various cells formed, each one takes on a specific function. Each and every cell knows how to grow further and how to synchronize with other billion cells to make a complete human body. These cells make the baby's spinal cord, the bones, the arms, the legs, the brain, the lever, the kidneys, millions of blood vessel, eyes, ears, nose, the heart, not only in static form but finally making it beat in the right rhythm and the seamless skin covering the entire body, without any marks or joints.

The human brain contains 100 billion neurons approximately, (also called nerve cells or brain cells), which is about the number of stars in the Milky Way Galaxy. The brain grows at the rate of about 250,000 nerve cells per minute, on an average, throughout the course of pregnancy. The development of the complete human body is an extraordinarily complex project on an extremely tight schedule.

Bill, can you imagine how such an intricate network is created and processed.

As per my discussion with a doctor he said, the sperm and the egg, which combine as one cell, they only take blood from mothers' body i.e., they take only energy from the mother's body, but as far as the intelligence in concerned, it is already contained in the cell. The intelligence does not come from any external source.

The doctor said, "We have not been able to know even one percent about the intricacies involved in the complete process during pregnancy. If we were knowing, we would have easily made various body parts. But the fact remains, we are poles apart from knowing the miracles, nature is conducting during formation of a human body. The complete process of human body creation is ineffable."

Bill just with a handful of knowledge we are gloating with pride. But the cell, which is billion times smaller than our brain, has its own intelligence, the knowledge, and the capability to make the complete human body within nine months.

My Question is Bill.

- From where do these cells get their knowledge to perform such a formidable task so easily, precisely and smoothly without taking any external help?
- Form where do these cells get all their intelligence to make the various complicated and such diversified organs of human body?
- Who plans all this?
- Who monitors this convoluted chain of commands?
- Who gives instruction to billions of cells to perform their task so diligently, meticulously and with such synergy?

Bill, please answer the question."

Bill smiles and replies, "I understand your point, Steve. Your question is just like Newton wondering why the apple fell down rather than going sideways or even upward. His question gave birth to a stupendous discovery i.e., Gravity. Similarly, Steve, if a man goes so deep as you stated, he would culminate into the discovery of the one and only one i.e., God. But only a Yogi would think in such a manner, not a common man.

I do accept Steve that there is a supreme power behind all this. Your assertion about God's existence is incontrovertibly true. Probably I can deny my existence but not God's."

Steve continues, "Bill there are seven wonders in the world which we admire made by man. But have we ever paid attention to this wonderful Universe. Bill, just look all around you, this planet is having millions of different species, half on earth and half in water, millions of plants and trees, fruits, flowers etc. and everything happening in a magnificent way. Is this all not marvelous? Unfortunately, we ignore to acknowledge this magnificent creation and we think there are only seven wonders on this earth, whereas if you ask me, every creation of God is a magnificent piece of art. When you see a mobile phone, the intricate work arouses our praises for the manufacturer, when we see the huge airplanes, the space shuttles, the satellites, the skyscrapers it causes us to marvel at its advanced engineering, but when we see the creation, then why do we become so vacuous and dull. Is it not our sheer ignorance.

Just imagine, how the soil transforms into millions of different trees, with different colors, shapes, fruits, into different plants and flowers with all its fragrance and beauty, into different kind of food for the millions of species on earth. How millions of liters of water transform into vapor, holding itself in the sky without any support and then this huge quantity further showers on earth so gently. How does the sunlight reach earth so precisely, how does the earth which hurtles through the space around the sun at a velocity of 107,000 km/h, does not make any sound or vibration.

Bill if you go deep into this cosmos, you will find everything referring indirectly to the one and only one i.e., God. Now you can call it God, consciousness, nature, the supreme power, the supreme intelligence, the ultimate source, the soul, the spirit, whatever you can. All are simply different names of one supreme entity. Unfortunately, human being has remained confused since ages in this matter.

However, once you are awakened and enlightened, all your confusion will be obliterated and you will have the ultimate realization of the One Creator, which has no name, no religion, no caste, no gender, no age, no shape, no color. He is imperceptible, omnipotent, omnipresent. He is the one and only one "God."

"Bill is it clear?" asks Steve.

"Ofcourse Steve, very much. The way you have described with your incisive words, there is not a scintilla of doubt about God's existence and His miracles. His existence is an irrefragable truth and I believe with certitude. Only an ignorant can deny Him, but not the wise. Please continue Steve," says Bill.

Steve says, "OK Bill let me move forward to the next point. How to find God or the ultimate source of this whole creation."

Steve continues.

"Bill scientists are trying to reach to the ultimate source from where the big bang started. However, even if science manages to reach to the source, it would be futile, as the scientists would not be able to find anything."

"Why Steve?" asks Bill.

Steve replies, "This is mainly because the source has already evolved. I would like to explain this phenomenon with a small example. Listen to me carefully Bill. Just like a seed which has now evolved into a tree and the tree has further evolved into many different forms like its trunk, branches, leaves, flowers etc. Now the seed has manifested itself into the complete tree. The seed is no longer available at the source i.e., at the roots. The seed is now there within the fruits of the tree. Similarly, the source of this creation has manifested itself into the complete Universe and the ultimate fruit of this Universe is the "**Human Being**." Now that source lies within each and every human being.

He is there within us Bill.

So even if the scientists manage to reach to the source of the big bang, in this profound Universe, they will find nothing, it will be a futile effort.

Bill now answering your Question, who are we?

We are not just a body, the product of the five elements water, earth, air, fire and space as the science defines. We are the divine beings. As I told you, the answer would be incomplete if I would take reference from science. In order to give you the right answer I have to take reference from a spiritual perspective. We are basically the divine beings, in human form, experiencing a small part of God's creation, with our limited intellect and ability.

As the French philosopher Pierre Teilhard de Chardin says, "**We are not human beings having a spiritual experience; we are spiritual beings having a human experience.**"

Bill, we are the key to the journey, we are the ones who have the access to that ultimate source of creation, we are those species having the immense treasure within us, we are not just a creation, we have the entire creation within us. The ultimate reality, the ultimate source lies within us, and we human being have been privileged to access that source unconditionally and entirely. We are not just body, neither bones nor flesh, we are not the mind, the feelings or just the thoughts or emotions, we are not what we believe, we are way beyond the definition of science and much beyond what we apparently look or the way we identify ourselves.

We are the One in which everything is rooted, the spark, the spirit, the bliss, the power, the wisdom, all the beauty, all the creation, the paradise, ultimate destiny and the infinite is within us. This is a journey of experience, a journey to think above all the science and logic, a journey of awakening and finally a journey of self-realization. We are all just One, in various forms. We consider ourselves to be different, out of our ignorance, but the fact is we are all One, from the One and within the One.

Unfortunately, we all fail to recognize ourselves truly. This is the irony of human life.

Bill, I suppose I am clear?" asks Steve.

"Yes Steve. I can comprehend what you mean to say." replies Bill.

Steve continues, "Well now the questions is how to find that source. What is the exact way to find that source. Before I give you the answer Bill, we have to understand that God is not an object. He is not someone that is sitting far away in some kingdom and ruling over everything. He is not physically away from you. He is omnipresent, He is everywhere. Basically, it's like air which is ubiquitous. To reach air you don't have to travel somewhere. You just need to breathe, and the air is felt within you, giving life to you. Similarly, to reach God you don't need to go to the forest or to the mountains or abandon your family, you just need to feel Him. There is no need to perform any practices which require extra ordinary physical endurance or to exhibit obliviousness to extreme physical conditions. This is not the criteria to commune with God. You just need to "**Feel**" Him everywhere. It is so simple Bill. Just try to **Feel Him, Feel Him and Feel Him**!!!

I hope you are getting my point. This may sound very surprising, but Bill this is true. You have to feel Him through your heart. The more you start feeling God from the core of your heart, the more you move closer to Him. Just feel God within you, all around you, within everyone and you will start becoming one with Him. This is the ultimate realization. The Bhagwad Gita says, "He who with devotion absorbs himself in Me, with his soul immersed in Me, I regard him, among all classes of yogis, as the most equilibrated."

What is meditation Bill? Meditation is not just to renounce God's name again and again. This is meaningless. Meditation means to feel God every moment as you are chanting his name, again and again. However, if you cannot feel God by chanting his name, then it is futile. Meditation will be meaningless. Every effort in spirituality or religion is to feel God more and more.

When you start feeling God, this feeling is not mutual between God and you, it is universal. Bill let me elaborate this point in more detail.

Bill when you are in love with someone, the feeling is mutual. Both the persons get immensely involved into each other. Most of the time people in love are musing over their love partners, they get absorbed into each other and consequently they get disengaged with others. Sometimes there will an ambivalent feeling between two lovers. Hence in love, people become possessive, they become obsessed, a feeling of anxiety also prevails due to fear of separation, also jealousy and possessiveness can lead to emotional imbalance. Moreover, in mutual love, everything seems to be banal after some time. All the spark and excitement start ebbing away as time passes. This is personal love, and the stark reality of personal love is that this mutual feeling is confided between two individuals, deeply rooted with expectations, gratification and sometimes with exacting demands. This feeling is reversible and also corruptible. Sometimes what seems like love, it can be limerence.

However, when you are in love with God, the feeling is Universal. Since God is everywhere and in everything, you become one with the whole creation. In love with God, your feeling is not confined to one religion, to one community, to one caste, to a certain class, to people of one nationality, it includes everything. It is like the fragrance of a flower that drifts through the air, naturally, unconditionally and indiscriminately. It integrates you with the whole creation, with nature, with other people irrespective of their religion, caste, gender, age, status, wealth, nationality etc. You will feel God in everything, in nature, in animals, in every human being, whether they are your enemies or your friends, whether they are strangers or relatives, whether they are good or bad, you will have no ill will against anyone in your heart. This is divine love, having no boundaries, limitless, unconditional, immutable, exquisitely blended with purity. Moreover, as you advance, the feeling becomes more intense, deep and you are wreathed with joy and fulfilment within your heart and soul.

Bill, once you experience this Universal feeling you cannot hurt anyone in this world. This feeling generates more compassion, love, empathy and understanding within you. It strengthens you, fulfills you, purifies you more and more. At this stage you don't hurt anyone, and you don't fear to get hurt by anyone. This Universal love is unadulterated. It is different from the standards of human love. There is no duality, there is no hypocrisy, you become one as a person, within yourself and with the entire creation. You become selfless. You feel one and completely united with the whole Universe. This is love with God, it is never personal, it is universal. It makes you more human, a better human and a perfect human.

This is the ultimate goal of human being and the ultimate "**Purpose of Human life**."

Bill, every human being may not be capable of becoming a good doctor, engineer, singer, athlete, businessman, a Hollywood star etc., but the Universe has given equal capacity to every human being to transmute himself or herself into the divine. As far as worldly skills are concerned there are diversifications, but as far as spiritual objectives are concerned, God has made us exactly equal, we all are equally privileged. We all human beings have the innate capacity to become divine at any stage of our life. Hence it does not matter whether you are rich or poor, you are educated or uneducated, you are young or old, you are sick or healthy, everyone has the privilege to become divine in his life.

Bill, I hope you are now clear about the creation. I hope you understand the ultimate purpose of human life."

"Yes Steve. It's very clear. Steve answer me honestly. Did you ever meet God? I think you have." asks Bill.

Steve replies with a smile, "No Bill I haven't. But I felt Him sometimes. Whenever I felt Him, I had this feeling. I had this strong Universal feeling. Bill as I told you, this feeling was never mutual it was Universal. What I am sharing with you is not the bookish knowledge, it is something that I have experienced immensely, whenever I tried to pursue God."

Bill replies, "Steve very eloquently and concisely you have shared your knowledge on such a recondite subject. The way you have explained about God, is phenomenal, I am thrilled Steve, especially the way you segue from one subject to another. I can listen to you whole night, the way you speak, so simply, so coherently, so clearly, each and every word of yours is so meaningful. I love to hear every little nuance of your philosophies. I am lucky to have you with me as my friend Steve. I can feel God through you. I can feel Him so near, through your words, the way you describe God, the way you feel Him so close, it gives me the same feeling. Steve, I think I am meditating while listening to you."

Steve smiles and says, "Fine Bill. I am happy you find all this so meaningful. OK Bill. There are only two questions left. Why this creation and why we human beings have become so insane and have put ourselves in such a pathetic situation.

So, Bill let me start with "Why this creation?"

This question has also perplexed human beings for centuries and will continue to do so. I was very much curious to know the answer. Wherever I went, this used to be my first question, unfortunately everyone equivocated on this matter. I read hundreds of books to get the answer. There are enormous theories on why this evolution happened and most of them are quite elusive.

However, after deep research and a nuance understanding about this topic, the answer which I learned, and which convinced me is as follows:

The objective of the entire creation is nothing but just a "**Passion**" of God. Bill this whole creation is His passion. Just like a singer, singing his song from his heart, unconcerned about the listeners, a painter making his painting, getting so involved as if the painting is the real world and everything else is an illusion, a saint spreading his love without any expectations, a flower spreading its fragrance, the clouds showering rain on earth indiscriminately, a mother sacrificing everything to raise her kids in the best possible manner, without any expectations, so is the whole creation. All is just an act of His passion. Millions of stars, galaxies, the sun, the moon, the earth, the sky are his paintings, the birds chirping so melodiously is His song, the life on earth with so much of diversities is His art of creation, the dainty flowers, the mesmerizing fragrance, the soft and vivacious beauty, is the garden of the Almighty Gardener. How everything comes from this soil and finally merges into the soil, is the mystery of that Magician. Human being, his ultimate creation, the closer to him, who can feel God, who has access to him, is His Masterpiece. The whole creation is just a passion of that one and only one Creator. There is no other reason of Creation. It's just His Passion, Passion and Passion!!!

Millions raised this question and asked why this Creation, but it remained inscrutable to everyone. However, the few who realized, they just merged into that One and only One, concluding that nothing is different in this world, everything is just One. What you see or conceive something other than you, is just illusion. However, when you elevate from this human body to the divine being, you will realize that everything is just one entity. Nothing is separate or nothing is against you, everything is within you, and you are within the One creator. You are the creation and you are the source.

Bill, this may sound difficult to understand, but that's how it is."

Bill says, "I understand. Steve, basically God is simple, but the creation is complex. However, the theories on God are also baffling, but the way you have described, it's very clear, intriguing and sublime. There is no room for any doubt. Your enlightening words has enlarged and vivified my perception of God and His creation. I really wished I could have known all this long before.

Good Steve. Excellent!!!"

Bill once again becomes pensive. After few minutes Bill asks, "Steve I am still confused with one thing. Why the masterpiece of God is in such a pathetic situation?

Why human being, such a sensible creation of God is found doing the most insane things in this world. Nothing in this creation is so awful as the deeds of human beings. As you said Steve, if we scale down the total time, since the inception of this Universe into 24 hours, then human beings have evolved only two seconds ago. Yet in that short time just imagine, how indelible mark we have left to the history of this creation, the bloodshed, damage to the environment and unfortunately the way humans have behaved so vilely, which has made them the most shameless and miserable creature on earth."

Steve replies, "I understand your point, Bill. Why human being the best creation has behaved in the most wretched way. Well Bill, as I told you everything in this Universe is integrated.

But now let me tell you precisely. Everything in this Universe is integrated except one thing i.e., Human mind.

There is a small story which is quite famous.

Once a professor asked his students in his class, "Is there a place where God is not present. The students were silent and surprised as they were always taught, that God is omnipresent and He is everywhere. However, the professor gave one day to the students to find the answer.

Although the professor knew what the answer was, yet he asked the question, just in a different way. However next day he again asked the students the same question. One boy raised his hand.

The professor asked, "Do you know that place where God is not present?"

The boy said, "Yes sir, there is one such place where God is totally absent."

The professor was awestruck and he said, "Fine then, please share that place where God is not present."

The boy replied, "God is present everywhere, except one place and that is, in the mind of the human being. We human beings, have everything in our mind, all the science, all the knowledge, our intelligence, our desires, our emotions, our priorities, our relatives, our friends, the whole materialistic and mundane world, but one thing what we have completely forgotten is "God." Unfortunately, our mind is the only place in this Universe, where God does not reside."

The professor was amazed, since the answer was correct, but contrary to his teachings.

So, Bill, the only thing, which is disintegrated with the creation, is our mind. All spirituality or religion is just to integrate this mind with God. Because of this disintegration, human being is doing all insane deeds, he is becoming the weirdest creature on earth and consequently facing all the pains, sufferings and is wandering in his entire life, with confusions and in despair."

Bill asks, "Steve but why human being is disintegrated?"

Steve answers obliquely, "I knew Bill, you would ask me this question. Bill, human being is the only creation of God who has been blessed with "**Free will**," the highest privilege any species has in this Universe. God has given free will only to human beings and no one else. Because of this free will, we make choices. All sorts of choices, good or bad, moral or immoral, to love or to hate, to forgive or to admonish, to act or to desist, to be sensible or to be insane etc. At every moment we have choices. Life is an event of choices for human beings. Animals do not have choices. A lion will die because of hunger but will not eat grass. A horse will die of hunger but will not start eating cats.

Bill, the mind of animals is like ROM in a computer. Read Only Memory (ROM), which is an integrated circuit programmed with specific data when it's manufactured. It's a non-volatile memory. The content of the ROM can't be altered, which means you can't reprogram, rewrite, or erase its content. This means, animals just follow their mind, without having any choices.

The mind of a human being is like RAM in a computer basically a volatile memory i.e., it temporarily stores files on which you are working on. It allows reading, writing. altering, erasing all operations. Hence human beings are at the liberty to reprogram their mind as per their choices. Since we have choices, we are accountable for our deeds. Hence, we reap what we sow and have to face the consequences. Accordingly, when we make bad choices, we suffer accordingly.

The crux of the whole issue is, since we have the privilege to make choices because of our freewill, the mind has gone haywire and finally disintegrated, with the one Creator.

For e.g., Bill, do you need to say to a cow, "Behave like a cow." Do you need to say to a monkey, "Behave like a monkey or to a donkey "Behave like a donkey" or to any other animal or bird. The answer is "No," "Never." However, to a human being you have to say hundred times, "Be a good Human" and still he fails with disgrace."

Bill laughs and says, "Good one Steve. You are right. Even to a donkey there is no need to tell him "Behave like a donkey," but to a human being we need to remind him again and again, and unfortunately, he still does not understand. How pathetic we human beings are."

Bill asks again, "But Steve, why is the mind disintegrated, can you give me a straight answer?"

Steve answers, "Bill, because of multitudinous distractions. As I told you before Bill,

"***The way human beings are knowledgeable today they were never before, unfortunately the way human beings are distracted today they were never before.***"

Steve continues, "Bill there are two types of distractions. One is negative and the other is positive.

Positive means, seeking pleasures from sex, alcohol, drugs, the titillating images on social media, fantasies, seeking recognition, power, money, fame, attachments with our family, our unscrupulous and endless desires for the materialistic things etc. These are all positive distractions.

The negative distractions are our ego, our negative emotions like lust, anger, greed, jealousy, hatred, enmity, criticism, filling our hearts with the flaws of other people, anxiety, fear, worries, depressions, immoral deeds, our sins, hidden secrets, restlessness, our setbacks, bad health, our poor slavish beliefs, our meaningless preconceived notions, bad company or bad circumstances, etc.

Bill, when we are young and energetic, we are quite vulnerable to get disoriented due to the positive distractions and as we grow old, we encounter the negative distractions. As a result, human being remains disintegrated throughout his life. Bill, since ages human being has remained distracted and in today's world, because of the advancement of technology and pervasiveness of personal digital devices like desktops, laptops, smartphones, tablets etc., which provide unlimited access to heaps of information, unresisting modes of pleasures and other privileges, human being is at the height of his distraction."

"Bill what is social media?" asks Steve.

"It's an online crowd," replies Bill.

Steve says, "No Bill, it's not an online crowd. If you recall my first story, social media is like the massive fair in which the boy got tempted with the toy and lost his mother. It's an agglomeration, where you have millions of people who converge for fun and frolic, where there is dance, music, entertainment, knowledge, information, news, myriad sources of recreation, opportunities, a virtual world which has virtually no end. It's a parallel world, a man-made world, more glamorous and more artificial. I call social media as a parallel world, which is basically a fair. A fair which is ridiculously huge, boundless, having no boundaries or limits. This massive fair is going on 24 hours and 365 days. There are multiple entry gates but unfortunately there is no exit. People who entered once, never came out. They got lost into the labyrinth of never-ending shows on the social media and remained lost forever.

Hence Bill, the way people are distracted today they were never before.

Bill, I think I am clear. I hope I have answered all your questions. Let us take a break here. We will continue again tomorrow with a new topic.

Bill says, "Well Steve, Great. It is one of the greatest days of my life. I feel like I have found some treasure today. Earlier my mind used to swing between confusion and despair, but now there is deep feeling of elation within me. I am feeling exalted, as if I am reborn. It seems I have found my true identity today.

I found the true meaning of life, I found my purpose, and the best thing is I found a true friend in my life, and now I feel as if, I found everything.

Steve, I recall the quote of the great Indian president Mr. Abdul Kalam "**One best book is equal to a hundred good friends, but one good friend is equal to a library.**" Today I feel that the quote is so true. Steve many thanks to you. I want to thank you again and again."

Bill's eyes are moist with tears now.

Steve smiles and says, "OK Bill I will take your leave now. Let's meet tomorrow. I would love to enjoy the coffee with some homemade Belgian biscuits, with you in the morning."

Chapter 5

THE ULTIMATE SAVER

It is morning. Bill and Steve are once again at their morning breakfast table.

Bill once again recalls all his childhood heartwarming memories. Those childhood events which were simple but so joyful like building sandcastles, climbing a tree, eating fish and chips, buying penny sweets from the village shop, the ice cream from the van shop, the school sports day, counting down the days until the summer holidays, the birthday celebrations, watching films, his first-time experience on an airplane during a family holiday trip, the excitement of Christmas celebration.

The Christmas holidays were the most un-forgetful memories of all. Decorating the Christmas tree that people adorn with lights, artificial stars, toys, bells, flowers, gifts, etc., visiting churches with families and friends, light candles in front of the idol of Jesus Christ, children longing for Santa Claus to arrive, the excitement and craze of receiving gifts, children performing pantomime on Christmas, family get-togethers, the neighbor who used to bake delicious cakes, seeing the decoration that spread all over the village, including the shops, the roads, each and every house in the village which was decorated with lights and stars, colorful balloons and flowers. Everywhere there used to be happiness, hope, love and joy, a magical festival, celebrated with so much of vibrance and vigor.

So simple were the celebrations, yet so lively, with intense warmth of love and positivity everywhere. There was nothing in this world more entrancing than these childhood days. Bill becomes scintillant with the recollection of endearing childhood memories.

However, after the breakfast Bill and Steve are back again in the library.

Bill says, "Steve I want to ask you one Question. Why do you have this beard and a moustache like a Yogi. Are you following some Guru or seeking some specific spiritual path in your life? You are an American, you used to be clean shaved. You looked like a handsome model, you were like James Bond. How such a change?"

Steve replies, "No Bill neither I am following any Guru in my life nor this beard is due to any religious or spiritual concern. There is a long story behind this."

Bill says, "I would like to know the story, Steve. Please tell me."

Steve says, "OK Bill. On your assignment I travelled all over the world except the Himalayas. Somehow, I missed visiting the Himalayas. However, I made it a point to visit it, whenever I got a chance.

After I quit my job from your company, I joined some other organization. After few years I took leave and planned to go to the Himalayas.

As planned, I went to India, I took a guide and we started our journey. The guide was quite experienced, and he gave me various options to explore the spectacular beauty of Himalayas in the best possible way.

We visited the Himalayas during the spring. I was thrilled to experience the serene exquisiteness of the Himalayas.

The sunshine was bright with soft and cold breeze, making the place like a paradise. I was enamored to see the charismatic meadows, lakes, rivers, lush valleys, the profusion of flowers, amazing flora and fauna, the stunning beauty of the magnetic hills and the majestic mountains of unfathomable scale. The pure, salubrious air, full of oxygen, the peaceful environment, mineral rich water, all making it a heaven like place on earth. The beauty of Himalayas was sublime and ineffable. This visit was a spiritual experience and it gave me invigorating respite from the daily monotonous routine of my life.

On the Himalayas at many places, we met several yogis, hermits, ascetics, sadhus, rishis etc. living in solitude and silence. Almost everyone had a long beard and a long hair. Some used to coil up their hair on the crown of their head and some let it loose scattered. I asked everyone why they grew this long hair, beard and a moustache and I got various answers from them.

Some replied that it was the way a yogi has to live, some said because the hair stores all their spiritual energy and also draws more energy to the brain, some said that it absorbs cosmic energy from ether, some also gave me a scientific explanation that certain vitamins and essential minerals are produced in the body once your hair on your head is allowed to attain its full mature length.

Whatever answers I received, I listened to them airily and was not satisfied. However, the journey to the Himalayas was very entrancing. It was a great experience for me to see nature in its permutation of beauty and also seeing that nonchalant reclusive and austere life of those ascetics in this modern world, totally isolated and living in their own joy and spirits.

I came back to U.S. on Saturday morning and took rest for the entire day to restore my vigor. On Sunday I was doing my shaving and suddenly I got a small cut on my face. Little blood oozed out and as usual I dabbed the cut with an antiseptic and it was perfectly fine. However, standing in front of the mirror, a question came to my mind, in a trice. The question was that while I was in India visiting the Himalayas, I never shaved. Most of the time my hair was disheveled and face was always unshaven. Those days were the most joyful days of my life, the happiest moments. So, the Question was, why was I shaving today?

For Whom?
For What?
Was I shaving for myself?
Was I shaving for happiness?
What is the reason?

The answer came very easily. I was preparing myself for the next day, to go to my office. I was basically preparing myself, the way people wanted to see me in the office. It was not for myself, it was for the people, my colleagues, my boss who would like to see me clean shaved. It was all because of them, I was doing the shaving.

One thing I realized Bill at that moment was, that not only do we dress, but we do everything in our life to please others, irrespective of how unpleasant and insignificant it is, to us. For e.g., a lot of ladies' wear heels, if you go and ask them, are they comfortable, the answer is "No," because the heels abnormally change your stance and push your bones in such an abnormal way, they aren't meant to be. This results into pain and one wrong step can be so perilous that it can even fracture your ankle. Still, they wear it.

A lot of people use hair dye, do they enjoy doing it, the answer is "No." They are aware of the terrible side effects of a hair dye, but still they do it, to look younger as compared to others. Just to show themselves on Facebook, Instagram and other such social media platforms, for appreciation.

Sometimes I used to feel very uncomfortable in my three-piece suit, but I had to wear it, during our formal meetings and sometimes during the evening dinners too. The most uncomfortable thing is to wear a necktie. Medically it has been proven that wearing a tight collar or tie may compromise the venous drainage of the brain. Wearing ties can make you look nicer in meetings, but it has consequences like headaches, neck aches, rashes etc.

However, the erudite class wear a full suit with a tie and this business attire is considered as a symbol of their seniority and education. Unfortunately, if someone does not wear it, people would regard him with contempt.

So basically, we dress to look as per other people's expectations and not the way we are comfortable. We are molding ourselves as per people's opinions, their standards, their comfort level, their hopes and anticipations. We have prioritized our life to the external unknown world and are trying to meet their standards unconditionally rather than considering to think intelligently, what is indeed good and bad for us.

Bill at that moment this thought clicked to me that I am preparing myself for someone else and not for me. However, this is not the way we are supposed to live. We need to live freely, for ourselves, we need to live comfortably, and not for the pleasure or under the influence and approval of others. Why should I give more priority to the comforts of others, rather than my own.

As long as I have a moral, ethical and a graceful life, I need not worry about the opinion of people. After few years when I left the job, I never shaved. I felt as if I was free. Completely free from within myself. I have given up all the embellishments and decorations, which make my life unpleasant and uncomfortable. Basically, I left slavery and hypocrisy.

Further Bill, I realized that the more you are closer to nature, the more you become natural. Our body is perfect and a masterpiece of this creation. Nature has not given anything which is not necessary in our body, not even a small microscopic cell. Our body is a perfect masterpiece of the Creator. It's not that I am following any religion or any spiritual path but now I am the way nature has made me. I look natural, I am comfortable with myself, I am happy with myself.

My friends were initially surprised but as I shared my experience and my feelings, they appreciated it, and they love me just like you."

Bill says, "Good Steve, Impressive. I understand Steve you are indeed free now.

I agree with you, it doesn't matter how people perceive us, what matters is that we should feel free from within ourselves. There is no need to follow this artificial world and their ambiguous and dubious standards. We should live the way we want to live, the way we feel comfortable. We should not get distracted by people's opinion, which becomes a barrier between us and our freedom, our happiness, our peace of mind. For e.g., fashion is the biggest barrier between our life and simplicity, and it is nothing just a dubious standard of this world. You are right Steve, we should free ourselves from these meaningless worldly norms which are endless, making us uncomfortable and restless."

Bill further asks, "Steve, I have a lot of questions in my life. Is it normal to have questions. Did you have any questions in your life?"

Steve replies, "Ofcourse Bill, a lot of questions."

Bill asks, "What kind of questions?"

Steve says, "Bill, before I give you the answer, I want you to tell me, why do people have questions in life?"

Bill replies, "I think Steve, people ask questions, to acquire knowledge, to clear their confusions, or to solve their problems, I think these are the basic reasons."

Steve says, "I agree with you Bill. You are right, people ask questions to acquire knowledge, to clear their confusions, or to solve their problems, but the nature of questions changes in different stages of life. There is something more which we need to understand.

For e.g., to a child, questions arise due to his inquisitiveness. A child is totally ignorant about this world and due to his ignorance, there is an unbridled curiosity to know things more and more. Hence a child will have a lot of questions about everything he sees or experiences. He will ask anything incessantly, without shame or shyness. He is quite bold at this stage to ask questions. He is very eager to know the answers. However, this inquisitiveness does not come from depth. It is quite superficial just like his laughter and cry.

The next stage is youth. Questions arise to a youth mostly because of his ambitions and innate desires. Most of the youth will have questions about materialistic world. Their questions will be intelligent and intriguing, arising from their sharp intellect, which is at an evolving stage, but will be oblivious to the facts of life. Young people will talk more about money, their future, possessions, jobs, opportunities, their ambitions and goals.

These questions will be money oriented and centered all around materialistic world.

Further some young people seek pleasure and entertainment in life. They want instant gratification and pursue them intensely. For e.g., when young boys and girls sit and chat, they will generally talk about movies, celebrities, sports, adventures, romance, music, jokes, having fun etc.

You will hardly find young people talking about spirituality, God or anything related to life and death. Even if they talk, it is ostensible.

Lastly, the matured ones, who have experienced life as a whole, who have experienced the materialistic world, who have seen this artificial world closely and deeply, who have fulfilled their desires, who have enjoyed all the privileges with which a human being is blessed. After such a vast experience they find everything futile, everything meaningless and they now confront loneliness. All materialistic achievements, all comforts, all luxuries, wealth and powers, they find it purposeless.

At this moment the right questions will arise, these questions will have depth, will have true meaning of life, just like Buddha. Such people are actual seekers of truth.

Bill, when a person of your age and caliber says, I have a lot of questions, I know the nature of your questions. Your questions will be based on life, on our existence, on this creation, on morality, about true happiness, about God, about life, about death, about life after death, about liberation, about the ultimate reality of this mortal world.

So, Bill everyone at your stage will have the same questions what you have now. Even I had those questions, Bill. There is nothing so strange about it."

Bill says, "Great Steve. Very clear. However, I am still curious to know what precisely your questions were and what were the answers. The most important point is from where did you get the right answers?"

Steve says, "Bill after roaming all over the world, reading all the holy scriptures of various religions, studying all the philosophies of the world, all the scientific theories, meeting a lot of enlightened people, I got all the answers one by one, based on my sapience.

Bill let me tell you the most important thing, it does not matter how many books you have read, or how many scientific theories you know, or how many holy scriptures are at the tip of your tongue, but as long as your mind is not pure, all your knowledge will get contaminated with your impurities. If you are a seeker of truth, you should first purify your mind.

A pure mind means, the one which is free from all the emotions, desires, attachments, ego and various belief systems as taught by this world.

I shall share one story with you in this regard.

Once there was a monk. As per his daily routine he used to go to a street with his alms-bowl allowing the devotees to make their food offerings. In one of the houses, lived a rich lady, gloating with pride, obsessed with her ego, envying her neighbors and always shouting at her poor maid. She also gave food to the monk. The monk accepted food from everyone, with humility.

One day the lady asked the monk, "You are a monk why don't you give me some divine knowledge. I would like you to share your valuable wisdom with me, since I give you the best food every day, compared to others."

The monk said, "Fine lady, tomorrow when I come and while you give me some food, I will share my divine knowledge with you."

Next day the monk came and that lady made some good pudding. As she was about to put the pudding in monk's bowl, she stopped instantly, as she saw there was filth in the bowl. She was aghast and asked the monk, "What is this, are you insane? Your bowl is full of filth."

The monk said, "You wanted me to give you some divine knowledge. So, this is your lesson. Till the time your heart is full with impurities like your ego, jealousy, greed, envy towards your neighbors, disregard towards the poor, it is like filth in the bowl. Even if I share my divine knowledge with you, it will contaminate within you, just like the pudding you made, will become worthless if you put it in my bowl, already full of filth. Hence first free yourself with all these negative elements, make your bowl (inner heart) clean and then I will pour the nectar of wisdom in it, which will find a pure place to blossom in your life."

So, Bill till the time we don't purify ourselves, it is futile to grasp knowledge. To realize the wisdom, our inner space should be empty from all the malice and impurities. Actual growth in life will only start from the purification of our mind and our Intellect."

Bill says, "Good Steve. I got your point. This is the reason that even the formal academic education fails in this modern world. Because ultimately the impurities within our heart they contaminate our entire internal system. Our mind gets inflicted with our sensuous desires, unbalanced emotions, lust, conceit, ego, greed, wrath, depravity. Once our internal system is smothered with all these defilements, all our academic knowledge fails miserably. That is why we find most of the educated people vainglorious, spiteful, corrupted, reprobate, doing unethical things, becoming selfish, arrogant, talking to their employees with brazen disregard and what not.

You are perfectly right Steve, first we need to eradicate these defilements from within ourselves and then the nectar of wisdom will find its place to blossom. However, Steve please tell me how to free our mind from such emotions, desires, attachments and our beliefs?"

Steve replies, "Bill, as far as our emotions, desires and our attachments are concerned, they are inflicted because of us. You can obliterate them if you remain steadfast and determined. The problem is with the belief system. People are quite sequacious and they believe, not what is true, but what they are made to believe, no matter how untrue, preposterous and disillusioned the belief is. Unfortunately, it is almost impossible to obliterate their beliefs. Beliefs are implacable.

Bill I will share with you, one true event from the history.

After Joseph Stalin came into power in the U.S.S.R., a campaign began, which severely prohibited all the religious activities and supported atheism i.e., nonexistence of God and espoused the materialistic philosophy. The U.S.S.R. was evolving into a highly regimented country against the religious people, who were considered as unconditional enemies. It was a despicable move and a woeful decision of U.S.S.R., that had terrible effect on the entire nation.

Stalin called for an unconscionable "Atheist five-year plan" in order to eliminate all religious expression in the U.S.S.R. It was declared that the concept of God would disappear from the Soviet Union. It was an abhorrent and a baffling plan.

All Muslim, Jewish, Christian and Buddhist clergy faced persecution. However, the main target of the anti-religious campaign was the Russian Orthodox Church, which had the largest number of devotees. Nearly all of its clergy and many of its believers, were either shot or sent to labor camps. Many religious buildings were demolished. It was intended to modify all the buildings of worship into cinemas and graveyards into parks.

Schools that were supporting religious theories were closed and church publications were prohibited. Teachers accused of not supporting the anti-religious campaign could be fired, and in most cases the authorities imprisoned or exiled them.

The despotic campaign greatly diminished the number of functioning churches in the country.

Several initiatives were taken to eliminate the faith in God and instead have their faith in the state. The Soviet leadership instituted measures to stop the celebration of Christmas and other religious feasts.

In the late 1930, being associated with the Church was dangerous. Even a brief visit to Church could mean loss of employment and irreparable career damage and even an arrest.

Massive number of believers were effectively imprisoned or sometimes executed for nothing, except overtly witnessing their faith.

Hence Atheism was very aggressively campaigned by all means. U.S.S.R. wanted to delude their people with the fallacy of atheism.

After years of this campaign, once a press reporter asked a youngster in the U.S.S.R., "What do you think about God?"

The youngster replied, "There is no God."

The reporter argued and said, "In the whole world millions of people believe in God. There were thousands of Churches in the Soviet Union itself before 10 to 15 years. Still in Europe and America people believe strongly in God."

The youngster asserted, "Yes, God may have been there in the U.S.S.R., 10 to 15 years ago, **but He has left now. He has gone.**

God does not stay anymore, in U.S.S.R. If you want to see him, then probably you have to visit Europe or America."

So, Bill, the youngster believed that God is like a human being, who left U.S.S.R. and probably staying in Europe or America.

Bill, the point is that we don't believe what is indeed right or wrong, but we believe what we are made to believe, irrespective of whether it is true or untrue.

So probably we can conquer our emotions, desires, our attachments, our ego but not belief system. Our beliefs are immutable and unfortunately this holds us back terribly in life."

Bill interrupts and asks, "But Steve, why can't we conquer our belief system?"

Steve replies, "Bill, this is mainly because of our Ignorance and a weak Character.

Because of ignorance we do not have the sapience to reason it logically. Secondly, with a weak character, people don't have the courage to act on truth with certitude and abandon our worthless beliefs. Hence, we are encapsulated with such baseless beliefs, throughout our life.

Bill, for a youngster he considers his Character to be strong if he can ride his car or bike very fast, or if he has more muscles than others, or if he can impress girls better than others, or if he can drink more beer compared to his friends in a party. For a grown-up man, he thinks he has a strong character, if he earns more money than his contemporaries or if he has a bigger car, a bigger salary, a bigger post or a bigger house.

For a spiritual leader he thinks he has a strong character if he has all the knowledge of all the holy scriptures, or if he knows a lot of stories about God, or if he is a good orator and can attract thousands of people in the congregation through his sanctimonious speeches.

Bill, these are the general factors which various people consider to analyze their character, which are all meaningless, baseless and entrenches people with conceit. By meaningless factors we analyze our character and make our life totally worthless.

Bill, a strong Character does not come with such worthless features, it comes only with wisdom, purity in your heart, clarity in your vision, a life based on higher goals, probity, integrity and finally the courage to act on all your wisdom.

Bill today in certain situations people know what is right and what is wrong, but despite knowing the truth they don't have the courage to act on it. They become effete and dull. People falter even in noble solutions, just because they lack courage.

Bill we are internally impotent. We are selfish. We all lack the courage to remain steadfast or committed to the moral values and ethics on which humanity is based. On the other hand, when we are ignorant, we lack the courage to admit this truth. This is mainly because our ego does not allow us to admit our flaws, our deficiencies, our weaknesses. This is what our Character is today.

Without a strong Character people will have a very weak mind set and they become gullible. Once they are in a position of despair or despondency, you can trade their faith with anything meaningless. Unfortunately, this is happening everywhere in the world. People with problems wander here and there and if by chance their problems get resolved from somewhere, they can be made to believe anything, no matter how meaningless, how worthless, how preposterous those beliefs may be. This is how people develop blind faith in life.

All blind faith is a result of a person's ignorance and a weak mind set. However, this will not happen with a person of a strong Character."

Bill says, "I agree with you Steve. Just a few days ago, when I was in total despair and disillusion, I was in a very vulnerable situation. Anyone could have manipulated my mindset and could have taken undue advantage of me. I had no clue of life or truth, I was totally lost, I was directionless, I had no idea what to do. I lost my sapience. I suppose this is what people face in their lives.

You are right Steve, life is fragile and precarious at every moment of your struggle, and till the time we don't have the wisdom, the basic understanding of life, any knavish person can manipulate our mindset and repudiate or espouse any belief for his benefit. Our beliefs based on ignorance and a weak character, ossify on the long run, and make us blind. This is how I suppose people have blind faith.

So, Steve what happens when people have blind faith?"

Steve replies, "**When people have blind faith, then most of the times their faith is under the direction of those who themselves are blind. Finally, your situation will go from bad to worse.**

This is the irony of this world.

Our slavish beliefs keep us in thralldom and restrict our spiritual and mental growth. Bill what I am doing with you from last one week is that I am trying to break the fetters of your emotions, desires, attachments, ego and your slavish beliefs.

Bill you are already a strong man. You are very confident, you are tenacious, you don't fear failures in life, you are very enthusiastic, you are optimistic, you know how to take care of your challenges in the right way.

Bill, don't underestimate yourself, you are not a person who became rich by luck, you have merits, you have devoted your heart and soul into your work, you were a man of stupendous stamina and energy, you were very assiduous in your work, you have the charisma in you, you have the ability to influence people, your critics, your opponents, you can easily figure out solutions to your complications. Bill don't let that Bill die within you. Don't disparage yourself or wallow in self-pity.

Bill you were a person who could dare to fight alone, against millions, you had that fire, that vehemence within you. You fought your external struggles easily, now it is time to fight with your internal challenges. I have come here to wake that man up, that strong man, who never got depressed no matter how terrible the challenges were. I want that Bill to rise again.

Bill don't give up just because of the fear of death. Death can only take away your body but not your spirit, your spirit to live, your spirit of fearlessness, the energy and exuberance that pervades in your soul."

Steve's voice is gaining pitch and he continues.

"Bill, get up and prove what you are, you are strong and nothing in this world can defeat you. I always extolled your dynamism and your indomitable spirit, your courage. I learnt a lot from you. Sometimes you were my inspiration especially when you alone used to face the problems which seemed unsurmountable, but with your unflinching grit and determination, you conquered them alone. You are not a handful of dust lying at the mercy of the wind, you are a rock, and no one can easily turn you down. You are peerless. Wake up Bill, wake up !!!"

Bill is totally dazzled. His eyes are glistening with tears but also gleaming with satisfaction, there is a spark in his eyes, fulfilment in his heart, there is now a new stream of energy in Bill. Bill's countenance lit up and seemed illumined.

Bill says, "Thanks Steve. Thanks for everything. Do you really mean what you said?"

Steve replies, "Ofcourse Bill. You know I never lie in my life. I never exaggerate. I just say what I mean from the core of my heart."

Bill could feel that Steve's admiration is unfeigned and not a contrived praise.

Bill says, "Steve I don't have words for your moral support. Thanks for reminding me about the great personality that I was, which sometimes I also used to admire in the mirror, but Steve that person is evanescent. Gradually that personality started fading away in the mirror. One day I lost him somewhere. My identity is becoming more and more tenuous. That Bill is nowhere in the mirror now. I try to search him but cannot find him anywhere. Steve, I think I lost him somewhere."

Steve says, "It's simple Bill, in the mad rush of this world, you did not give time to your own self, and you lost that person within you, who was the real Bill, who was the hero. In the tedium of the daily mundane things, you lost him. If you had given proper time to him, he would have been still with you. Don't worry Bill, he has gone nowhere, he has been lying unattended within you. Now give him the opportunity to rise, move forward and fight the battle."

Bill speaks in a sanguine tone, "Yes Steve. You are right. I need to awaken that Bill within me, to whom I never gave any attention. Today I see that Bill through you Steve, I feel him now, I think he is alive in me, I feel the strength, I feel the spirit."

Bill feels highly motivated. He once again becomes pensive but seems very positive. Steve gets up and is looking for some books. He gives some time to Bill for cogitation. He wants Bill to realize his inner strength. Bill is already becoming confident day by day. However, with this motivation Bill's morale has received a tremendous boost.

After some time, there is a call for lunch.

Bill and Steve go for the lunch. They have a good time enjoying their meals. Steve is a finicky eater, very choosy. However, Bill has arranged for all those dishes which Steve relishes the most. Steve enjoys his meals. He appreciates Bill's hospitality and his concern for taking so much of care.

After the lunch Bill and Steve are once again back in the library.

Bill asks, "Steve I still have a lot of questions."

Steve says, "Go on Bill. Tell me what they are."

Bill asks, "Why are people scared of death?"

Steve replies, "Bill this is a very important question. Everyone is scared of death. Even I was terribly scared. However, as I realized certain truth about death, this atavistic fear diminished. I shall share with you the facts very briefly.

Bill there are three important things about death, which you need to know.

The first is, death is inevitable, which means death is certain, the second is the time of death, which is uncertain, and the third is the nature of death, which means how the death will come, whether as a disease, in an accident, in pestilence, in an ICU, in distress condition or in the arms of your beloved, in the memory of God or in a glorious way. No one wants to die in grief and vexation. We all know that one day we are all going to die, but the thing which bothers everyone is the nature of the death and its time, both of which are uncertain and unheralded.

Further Bill, the fear of death is a sign which shows your attachments with the materialistic world. The more we are elated with materialistic possessions, the more we are afraid of leaving it. Here, where spirituality comes into picture.

Death has its significance only in this mortal world, which means you fear it, as long as you are attached to your body, your family, your relatives, your wealth and this materialistic world. But in spiritual world death has no significance.

A rich person who lives in luxuries, owns several cars, houses, several factories, businesses will be more attached and entangled into this world. However, a poor person, who is living in a dilapidated house, does not have proper means to survive, will not fear death, like a rich man.

A young man who has friends, has a family, a home, a car, has wife and small children, has unaccomplished dreams, will be more attached to this world compared to an old man, who has reached the end of his tether, enfeebled with the mental and physical infirmities in his dotage, to whom no one pays any attention, whose most friends have passed away, who has no dreams to be accomplished, life is without any meaningful activity and life seems to have come to a halt or an impasse. Hence an old man would not be so afraid of death, as a young man.

A common man, who is ignorant about life and its purpose, in his old age will feel like a passenger, stranded on the platform, waiting alone for the train, having no clue of his onward journey. His mind may be in thrall of morbid fantasies.

However, a person who is spiritually enlightened, does not find himself alone, he is aware of his onward journey and is excited to move on. He knows death is nothing but a transition, it is the final truth of life, final destiny of every human being, and it's a part of the journey. Death is the ultimate liberation.

The legendary saint "Kabir" born in India during the 15th century says,

"**The whole world is scared of death, but I feel excited, because death is the opportunity for me to irrevocably commune with God**."

So, one way Bill death is not a problem. Let me conclude this in a simple way as I always say in my Quotes.

"Everyone is going to die one day. Don't worry, Death is never a problem, it's always the life."

I hope you understand the point Bill"

Bill says, "Yes Steve, very clear. You are right, it is not the death which causes the problem, it is the life. So enlightening Steve, please continue."

Steve says, "OK Bill let me share with you a funny story.

Once a noble saint used to ask a bright young man named Charlie, that he should come to the Church and meditate God as He is the ultimate objective. The young man said, "I agree with you but right now I have my priorities to study and complete my graduation. Once I complete my studies, I shall definitely follow your advice."

The young man completed his graduation. Once again, the saint met him and told him, "Since you have graduated now, you can start coming to the Church during the congregation."

Charlie having excelled in his academic studies replied smugly, "Yes, I would like to, but I just got a good job and I am also in love with a girl. I go every morning and evening to meet her. Soon we are going to get married and after my marriage, I will start coming to the church."

Charlie got married and after a couple of months once again the saint persuaded him.

Charlie said, "We are now expecting a baby, once the baby is born, I will start coming."

Well Charlie never went to the church. In a couple of years, he had three sons. Coincidentally the saint once again met Charlie and as usual requested him to come to the church.

Charlie replied offhandedly, "I have recently opened a new shop. I am quite busy. Once my business is set, I will start following as you say."

Time passed away very quickly, Charlie's sons grew up and started taking care of the business affairs of the shop. Charlie got very old and finally a day came when his life was approaching an end and he lay on the bed. The doctors declared that he would die any moment and suggested calling all his relatives, so that they can meet him for the last time.

All relatives gathered and advised Charlie to remember God, during his last moments.

Charlie being impervious to the relative's advice replied airily, "Don't worry, I will remember God."

However, after few seconds Charlie retorted, "Where are my sons?"

The wife replied, "They are with you. See on the left side your younger son is standing with you."

Charlie asked, "Where is the elder one?"

The wife said, "He is on the right-hand side."

Then Charlie asked, "Where is the third one?"

Wife again replied, "In front of you, can't you see?"

Charlie was confounded at his wife's answer and he shouted, "If three of them are here who is on the shop. Is the shop closed? You rascals, you are losing sales, losing money, go open the shop and send me the statement of profit and loss."

The relatives were baffled at such a ludicrous attitude of Charlie.

Bill chuckled and said, "Steve I love your exotic stories."

Steve says, "Bill we are so entangled in our worldly affairs that we have lost the slightest clue, that we are going to leave everything behind one day. Nothing is going to come with us. But we are so ignorant and so foolish that we have completely forgotten the ultimate destiny of life."

Bill says, "Steve I agree with you. I have gone through this phase in my life. We live as if we are immortal, we are emotionally attached to inanimate objects, we are senselessly sensitive to matters that are indeed worthless, and finally we are penny wise and pound foolish."

Bill continues, "Steve, tell me what is the most important thing in this whole Universe?"

Steve says, "Bill, before I give you a direct answer, I would like to ask you one simple question, which would probably urge you to find the right answer."

Bill excitingly asks, "Please ask Steve?"

Steve says, "Bill what is more important "**The Creation** or the **The Creator?**"

Bill smiles and says, "Of course The Creator!!!"

Steve says, "I hope you got your answer."

Bill says smilingly, "Very good Steve. I am enthralled by the way you clarify my confusions."

Steve continues, "Bill, there is small story which I learned when I was in India. An Indian Sanskrit Professor shared this intriguing story, with me. Probably this story would enlighten more on this subject."

Steve continues, "Long ago, a man named Abhi was held by the law keepers for his transgressions. The entire case was sent to the king. In those days, the kings used to give the judgements.

After studying all the facts, the king told Abhi, "I have studied your entire case and I have come to the conclusion that you are guilty of the crimes you are accused of. Hence as per the law, I have to convict you for life imprisonment. Abhi was aghast and he requested the king that though he was at fault, but he was ignorant about everything. He admitted his crimes and requested the king to exonerate him. However, the king was strict in the enforcement of law and known for his infallible justice.

Abhi once again implored and made a suppliant request for the sentence to be condoned.

The king, who was very strict but also magnanimous and known for his forbearance, thought for a while and told Abhi, "There is a provision in the law, that if any of your friends can come and give me an undertaking, I can acquit you for all your transgressions."

Abhi surprisingly said, "Is that all. You just need an undertaking from one of my friends and you will release me?"

The king said, "Yes, I will do, as the law says."

Abhi said, "I will go right now to my best friend and he will be here within few minutes with whatever undertaking you require."

The king said, "There is no hurry, you have twenty-four hours. You can bring your friend till tomorrow before day close. Once he gives me the undertaking you will be released and acquitted from all the charges."

Abhi was quite relaxed. He had a childhood friend, who was very near and dear to him. They have been studying together, playing together, spending hours together every day, the bonding was very deep and intense. Abhi immediately started for his friend's house.

As Abhi approached his friend's house, both of them saw each other from a distance. Abhi was happy to see him. As Abhi went nearer to the house, his friend went inside and the doors and windows got closed immediately. Abhi knocked the door, but there was no response from inside.

Abhi raised his voice asking for help and saying, "I am Abhi, your childhood friend, please open the door, I am in a big trouble. I want your help. If you don't help me, I will be ruined. I have no place for support. Please open the door." Still there was no response.

Abhi continued calling his friend, imploring again and again, lying whole day in front of the door. After receiving no response and in total dismay, Abhi finally burst into tears. Despite all the crying and whimpering, still there was no response. Abhi, finally realized that his friend has deceived him. Abhi who was totally exasperated and not able to fathom the spiteful behavior of his friend, backed away from the house.

Abhi, scared of the imminent punishment, rambled here and there. Suddenly he remembered a friend of him, to whom he used to meet occasionally. He was not very dear to him, as they used to meet only on special occasions, he was only an acquaintance. However, having no further options, Abhi decided to approach him. By the time he reached, it was dusk.

Apprehensively, Abhi knocked the door. His friend opened the door and seeing Abhi in such a distraught condition, got surprised. He asked Abhi, "What happened? Why this long face?"

Abhi answered morosely, "I am in big trouble I want your help."

The friend said, "Don't worry, I will try to help you, but it seems, right now you are totally worn out, you have not eaten anything. First come, sit with me, have a glass of water, I will get you something to eat. Once you settle down, tell me your problem I will try my level best to help you."

Abhi was quite relaxed and exulted. The friend offered him good food and then listened to Abhi about his entire problem, very compassionately.

Abhi blurted the whole incident to his friend and finally requested him to come to the king and provide the undertaking or else he would be imprisoned for his entire life.

Abhi's friend understood the problem and replied, "I understand your problem Abhi. But since this is related to the king, I am sorry, it is out of my reach. I have some limitations and I cannot give the undertaking. It is difficult for me to explain you why, but I am indeed sorry, this matter is beyond my authority. If there is anything else, please let me know."

Abhi was once again faced with disappointment. It was late night, Abhi came back home. While coming back, he appreciated that atleast this man welcomed him, listened to him properly, comforted him, but unfortunately, he also turned out to be of no help.

Abhi who was now restless and addled, could not sleep the whole night. Now he had no other friend to whom he could approach. In the morning, very disturbed and totally incapacitated, suddenly Abhi recalled a friend whom he met long ago. Unfortunately, Abhi never reciprocated or extended any courtesy to him. He had approached Abhi several times, but Abhi always ignored him. Having no other options left, Abhi thought of approaching him, as his last resort. He went to this friend's house in the morning with trepidation and without any hopes.

The man was sitting in his house very calmly. When he saw Abhi, he greeted him with a smile and a friendly countenance. Abhi spoke in a low voice, "I am in a great trouble and I have come for your help."

He was quite amiable and replied, "Don't worry, have breakfast with me, tell me your problem and I will try to help you."

Abhi had breakfast with him, shared his problem with a voice laced with sorrows, and requested, "If you can come and provide the undertaking to the king, I would be exonerated, through your intercession."

The friend replied, "Is this all that you want. Just one undertaking!!"

Abhi was quite surprised and said, "Yes, I want an undertaking from you and I would be acquitted from all the charges. So, are you willing to come with me?"

The friend replied, "Why not, let's go. As such I know the king very well, he is already a good friend of mine."

Abhi was surprised and happy that this friend has graciously acceded to help him, which was beyond his expectations. Abhi now took him to the king's court. There were guards, posted outside the palace. The guards looked at Abhi with a frigid stare but the moment they saw his friend, they reverently bowed their heads and gave way. Abhi was astounded to see, as the guards made their obeisance to his friend.

As they entered the court, another guard very obsequiously ushered them into the main hall, where the king was sitting on his throne, with all his ministers. As soon as the king saw his friend, he came running and bowed down to his friend and treated him with exceeding deference. Abhi was totally baffled and could not comprehend the worth of this man.

The king turned and told Abhi, "Is this the friend you were referring to, why didn't you tell me yesterday? I would have released you immediately. No undertaking is required now, your case is dismissed and you are released."

Abhi came out of the court. He was abundantly happy but quite disconcerted.

He wondered, "The person whom I ignored all my life, eventually helped me. All my other friends on whom I put my absolute faith, consequently proved to be useless at the time of need. However, the one, whom I thought was worthless and ignored all my life, turned out to be the most accomplished and influencing person in the whole kingdom. Had I made him my friend earlier I would have never encountered such a situation and would have also progressed by leaps and bounds. What a big naive I am. I did such a grave mistake in my life, in identifying the right person."

Abhi regretted his mistake.

The story ends over here. This story is an analogy to actual life.

Now the questions are:

Who is that man named Abhi?

Who is the king and who are those three friends?

The answers are:

That man named Abhi is a normal person like us, fallible beings. The king is the angel who records our good and bad deeds. Based on our deeds he gives his judgment.

What was the problem that Abhi had? The problem was death. As soon as we die the soul is presented in the court of God and the angel of justice studies our good and bad deeds and passes the verdict.

Who are those three friends?

The first friend who was a friend since childhood is the physical body. As soon as the human being dies, the body leaves the soul. The soul and body who were one on earth, are separated forever. However, the soul after leaving the body, turns back towards the body again and again but the body does not respond. The soul cries and shouts but the body is dead and is totally impervious to the soul. This body in which the soul had been residing for so many years, a whole life, suddenly closes all the doors and windows and the soul is unable to re-enter into this body. The soul is unable to comprehend this situation. At last, the soul leaves the body which is a very painful event for the soul.

The other friend:

The other friend is our relatives. Once a human being dies, they cremate the body, perform all the necessary rituals and finally pray for the departed soul. Unfortunately, beyond this, they have no access to help the soul. The soul having no support from the body now seeks support from the relatives, but unfortunately, they don't have access in the other world. They do want to help the soul, but they have their limitations. They can only pray and do nothing else.

The third friend:

The third friend who eventually helped, is "**God's name**." The One to whom we have ignored all our lifetime. In our entire life, we are busy in all our worldly affairs, but the most important task, is our connection with God. We never paid attention to it.

Bill, now a days people have millions of connections over Facebook, Instagram, LinkedIn but do we have any connection with God. The problem is that in our daily affairs and other priorities we have missed the most important thing, our connection with the source.

Bill, this is just like a woman who made fish curry for her husband. She was very excited to make the fish curry. She put very good spices, all different herbs, flavored it richly and made the fish curry very delectable. It was served in the best crockery. However lastly, she realized that there was something missing in the dish. The thing which was missing, was the fish. So is our life. We have put all the spices in our life, flavored it with all the materialistic things, but the main ingredient is missing in our life i.e., God. Finally, we end up into a rueful state.

So, God's name which is the panacea to all our problems and providing a never-ending support at every moment of our life, has been ignored by us all the time. It is the only thing which helps us everywhere, here in this mortal world and also in the world beyond, where the soul makes its final journey. The only resort is God's name. Unfortunately, we are naive and imbecile to realize this ultimate truth of life."

"Great story Steve!! Your stories are very intriguing. They are both thoughtful and informative. However, Steve I would like to know what do you mean by God's name, shall we meditate on him all the time?" asks Bill.

Steve replies, "God's name means, to connect with Him through love and awareness. God's name means to remember God, the one who is the creator of the whole Universe. When you remember him with love and through an awakened mind you will get more closer to him. God's name does not mean to recite his name physically or just mechanically. That will lead you nowhere. God's name means, when your mind is awakened, your heart is filled with love and your soul is empowered with purity, to finally commune with God."

Bill interrupts and asks, "Steve, you mean meditation. God's name means, should we meditate daily by chanting his name?"

Steve replies, "No Bill, not exactly meditation. I don't mean to say that you should sit every morning and chant his name again and again. This kind of meditation may be quite artificial. Till the time you are not deeply connected with God your meditation will not have any depth. Without depth, there would be no concentration and it would be burdensome on your mind. What I am trying to say is connect naturally with the supreme, without force. The real meditation is when you merge with the One through your awareness. Through awareness, there will be a keen understanding, this understanding will lead to much deeper connection with God. The deeper the connection, lesser will be your efforts to remember God or meditate upon Him. Finally, you need to reach to a stage, where with zero efforts you can concentrate, which means without any mental exertions or any strenuous efforts. I will share few examples with you Bill.

Bill, when I get up in the morning, I thank God for a wonderful morning, the strength which my body has regained to start with a new stream of energy and vitality. This is the first part of my meditation. When I go for a walk sometimes in the park, sometimes in the woods, sometimes in my garden and when I see the beauty of the nature, the morning sunlight, the cool breeze, the chirping of the birds, the fragrance and the vibrant colors of the flowers, the large expanse of the sky, I cannot help praising the glory of the Almighty God, this is my meditation. When my neighbors wave their hands smilingly and lovingly, I see God in them. When I go to my office and get involved in my work so much that I forget everything, however I thank God who gave me this ability to perform my duties with all the devotion, just the way I like to serve people in Church. I thank God for imparting all that intelligence, all the strength, all the skills, all the capabilities, this is my meditation.

When I get an opportunity to give something to the poor and the needy, I thank God for making me an instrument and a small part in the act of His benevolence. During my trying times, God helped me sometimes like a miracle or sometimes indirectly through some good people, I thank God for everything, this is my meditation. I thank God, for all the abilities, to make me think clearly and wisely in my life, I thank him for my wife, my children, my house, the food, the job, my friends, my neighbors, every moment that I lived smilingly, laughingly, lovingly, even those moments of my struggle, challenges, which were hard on me but they were important to make me strong, to make me wise, to make me humble, to understand life more closely, to enlighten me, to make me more balanced, stoic and matured. Bill every moment of my life is meditation.

My whole day goes in meditation, my life has become meditation.

I do sit chanting his name every day for a few minutes, but I don't fix a timeline, I don't chant his name forcefully or try to concentrate in some darkness. I meditate in the light of His glory, His love, His compassion, my sincere appreciation and gratitude for Him. I never tried to concentrate Bill; it all comes naturally. The more I understood the merits of Lord, the more I could feel Him and the more strongly get connected to Him, very naturally.

Every moment I see God in every act of my life, everywhere around me, in the whole creation.

Bill when you are awakened to this truth, you will realize that the supreme energy is pervading everywhere and at every moment. Consequently, your connection becomes deeper.

The stage of meditation which an ascetic is trying to achieve through strenuous efforts, is nothing compared to the meditation that a person is performing in an awakened state of mind, while performing his earthly duties conscientiously. A man having the responsibilities of family, working for the welfare of the society, fulfilling his obligations sincerely, and while doing all this, if he can still perceive God in everything, that person is the most elevated among all the Yogis in this world. This is the highest form of meditation.

Bill just by closing your eyes, forcefully stopping your thoughts, will never be fruitful. I don't mean to say that don't meditate by closing your eyes, but what I am emphasizing is, first awaken yourself. Right now Bill, what you need is not concentration, you need awakening. Once you are awakened your meditation will start automatically.

Meditation is not concentrating forcefully, it should be like the music which you enjoy listening over and over again, meditation should be like your morning sleep which you enjoy the most, meditation should be like alcohol, which keeps you intoxicated for several hours, meditation should be like the natural fragrance of the flower which you would like to have with you for your entire day, meditation should be like the play of children who never want to stop it, meditation should be like the person you love to be with, till eternity. All this will happen only when you are awakened in life. Bill, right now I am trying to awaken you. During an awakened stage the moment you close your eyes, you will not encounter darkness, but you will feel and experience the light within you, the bliss, the ecstasy.

The outer world and the inner world of an awakened person, become the same. He neither gets disturbed by the distraction of the outer world nor by his internal ruminations. Such a person becomes balanced, he becomes matured in life, he becomes the epitome of truth. An awakened person has nothing to hide, he has no secrets, he has no guilts, he has no fear, he is the light and the more the light spreads, there will be more love, truth, compassion, brotherhood, serenity, goodness, and finally more harmony, peace and happiness in this world.

I hope you understand what I mean Bill."

Bill says, "Yes Steve. Great. Very enlightening. You are very clear in your subjects. There is simplicity, but there is depth in what you say. It is easy to grasp you. When you speak, I get deeply involved in your words. Your words are enlightening, they give me direction, they provide me clarity, I feel supported by your words. They provide me respite from all my frustrations and grief. I feel free from all my trials and tribulations. All the data of this world is worthless compared to these few enlightening words; you share with me Steve."

Bill requests, "Steve, lastly, I want to know precisely all those questions along with their answers, that you were curious to know. Can you share them with me?"

Steve says, “Of course Bill, but it’s too late now. Tomorrow I shall share with you all those Q & A. I think it’s time for you to take rest. We shall continue with the session tomorrow.”

Bill says, “Fine Steve. See you tomorrow.”

Chapter 6

WISDOM

Steve and Bill are once again together at the breakfast. Bill seems to be getting more energetic and today he is very enthusiastic.

Bill says, "Steve I had a very sound sleep last night. Quite rejuvenating. Generally, I am deprived of good sleep in my life. Hence, I normally wake up intermittently during the night and sometimes ramble aimlessly, due to no reasons apparently. But last night it was like in a state of oblivion. I felt very energetic when I woke up. Mostly there are a lot of things in my mind when I wake up, but today, there was only one feeling, a feeling of gratitude towards God. I just thanked Him, for such a wonderful sleep and waking me up so energetically. I don't know how Steve, but I feel very good today."

Bill keeps on sharing his positive feelings. Steve is keenly listening. Bill is also enjoying the breakfast. After the breakfast Steve and Bill are once again at the library.

Bill as usual is very inquisitive for the Q & A and asks impatiently, "Steve I would like to know your question and answers."

Steve replies, "Bill I have brought all these Q & A with me. In one of my books, I have shared this eclectic Q & A as a conversation of a common man with God or say a common man asking some basic intriguing questions to God. In return God is furnishing laconic answers. I will read aloud all these Q & A. If you have any further questions, please let me know."

Bill says, "Interesting Steve. Please begin."

Steve starts sharing all the questions and answers:

Question & Answers with God

Man: Why is there so much of suffering in this world?

God: Every human being wants to become a Superhuman but not a better human.

Man: Is human being your best creation?

God: No, human being is my most advanced creation. To become the best or the worst, it depends on the deeds of every individual.

Man: Is there anything above human beings?

God: "Humanity"

Man: Why have you given only two hands to human beings. You know in today's world there is so much of work to be done and because of so much of work there is so much of stress. You should have given atleast four hands to human beings.

God: Two hands are enough to earn for your need but not for your greed.

Man: Why have you given only two legs to humans whereas you have given four legs to animals?

God: Because I want human beings to stand strong in all circumstances and not run like animals.

Man: Why have you given such a small heart in such a big body?

God: Your small heart is enough to love everything in this world including Me.

Man: Is there anything above religion?

God: Yes "Kindness." Kindness is the mother of religion.

Man: Which language do you speak or understand?

God: LOVE and AWARENESS. Rest all is insignificant.

Man: Do you value people's "Prayers"?

God: Yes, provided people value their own words.

Man: What kind of attitude you appreciate?

God: Give and Forgive.

Man: What is the root cause of sufferings in life?

God: "EGO" and "IGNORANCE."

Man: Sometimes when we pray with both our hands, still we do not get what we want. Why is it so?

God: Because people want to take with both the hands. Please keep one hand for giving and you will get in abundance from the other hand. No prayers will go in vain.

Man: If I want to help you what should I do?

God: Donate to the poor and the needy and share fairly what you have with the people who deserve it.

Man: How many candles shall I light to make you happy and my life, bright and successful?

God: Even if you light a million candles on my feet, but if you cannot perform your duties with all sincerity, honesty, dedication and serve your client with 100% loyalty, your life will be still full of darkness, giving no joy to me and making this world and your life darker than before.

Man: To get success for once, people fail hundred times. Why?

God: The enormity of success depends on the scale of your efforts and the magnitude of your failures.

Man: Why you are not visible?

God: If you can see your enemies with the same feeling as you see me, in my statue at the holy places, I shall be easily visible to you.

Man: Does anything impress you?

God: Yes, "Innocence and straightforwardness." People who are innocent and straightforward, they impress me.

Man: What is success and what is salvation?

God: To live with enthusiasm is success and to die peacefully without any desires, fear or stress is salvation.

Man: What is the ultimate path of Spirituality?

God: The ultimate path of spirituality is the path of living in present with your mind, body and soul as one, without the worries of future and infelicities of past.

Man: What are the signs of your blessings in a human being?

God: Humility, compassion and purity are the signs of my blessings.

Man: What is the difference between science and spirituality?

God: Science explores and gets connected to the creation while spirituality explores and gets connected to the creator.

Man: What is the meaning of success in materialistic world and spiritual world?

God: In materialistic world success means to become "Someone" and in spiritual world success means to become "No one."

Man: How can I empower my soul?

God: By purity and wisdom. Rest all is insignificant.

Man: If Birth and Death are not in our hands, then how come Life can be within our control?

God: The above statement is just like someone wondering,

That if my Height is not within my control, how can I control my Weight. "THINK DEEP".

Man: Will you meet me after I die?

God: Depends on how you live. If you don't desire me while living don't expect me after death. Death is the doorway which opens not towards the heavens but towards your own mindset. If your mind is pure, after death you will be in your own heaven, but if your mind is impure, you will be in your own Hell, after death.

Steve completes all the Q & A and says, "Bill these were the questions & answers. Do you have any other questions?"

Bill says, "Yes Steve, tell me how far is the saying 'Nothing is impossible' true?"

Steve replies, "Bill, "Nothing is impossible" is a good motivational statement. I appreciate it. However, this saying, still does not get you "Everything in life." I hope you understand this."

Bill says, "Very true Steve. Very true!!! OK Steve, tell me what are your views about Artificial intelligence?"

Steve replies, "Artificial Intelligence is nothing, but some advance logic based on algorithms without any "**Emotions**" or "**Awareness**." Artificial Intelligence is good to navigate a car but not human life.

Unfortunately, in this modern growing world, human beings are also becoming Artificially Intelligent.

Bill says, "Good Steve. Unequivocally true."

Bill further asks, "Steve, my last question. How do you perceive the future of this world?"

Steve replies, "If human being does not restrict his greed, the future of the world will be as follows:

1. As far as physical objects or gadgets are concerned, they will become more advanced and attractive.
2. As far as food, water and air is concerned, it will become more contaminated.
3. As far as human being is concerned, he will become more lonely and restless.

Eventually the next generation will have enough gadgets to play with, but scarce resources to survive and live peacefully."

Bill says, "That's pathetic Steve, but quite true."

Steve asks, "Any more questions, Bill?"

Bill says, "No more questions Steve for the moment."

Steve asks, "Bill I have one question for you."

Bill is surprised and asks, "For me Steve. What question?"

Steve asks, "Bill, tell me what is the major advantage to become the richest man on earth?"

Bill becomes pensive, takes a small breath and replies, "Steve, one of the major advantages of becoming the richest man of the world is, that you realize the worthlessness of excess money.

Steve, just as a child standing on the shore, to him it appears as if the sky and earth are meeting at some point, but a person who has already walked on that path, knows this is not true, it's an illusion. Similarly, to a poor person it seems, money would lead to all the happiness of this world, but if you ask to a person like me, who has walked the path would tell you, this is just an illusion.

Steve, chasing materialistic things for happiness, is just like chasing mirage for water, in a desert."

Steve says, "Very true answer, Bill."

Bill asks, "Steve I have one more question. How to come out of attachments of your family, your wife, your children. Probably you can get free from the bonds of your desires or the materialistic world, but how to get rid of these personal attachments. Is there a way?"

Steve replies, "Bill I shall share a small story with you. However, I suppose you have an appointment with your new doctor in a while and you will be busy with him. So, we shall meet tomorrow morning. I will share the last story with you. It will also be my last day Bill. I hope I have done my job. I feel that you are quite relaxed now."

Bill says, "Steve, I want you to be here with me all the time, but I understand that's not appropriate. However, I feel good. I feel much better."

Steve says, "Bill, don't worry about death. Before I leave, I shall cure your illness."

Bill is dazzled and asks, "What do you mean Steve?"

Steve says cryptically, "Bill, I will give you a small physical therapy that will cure your tumor."

Bill is totally non-plussed and looks quizzically at Steve.

However, Bill asks confusingly, "Steve do you mean to say you will cure my tumor with some therapy???"

Steve says, "Yes Bill."

Bill asks astoundingly, "What therapy Steve??"

Steve replies, "Bill, you leave all that upto me. I will do it. You know I don't commit, if I cannot do. So before I leave, I shall give you a small therapy and you will be cured."

Bill is totally speechless and staggered.

Steve leaves and Bill goes for his appointment with the new doctor.

Chapter 7

THE LAST STORY

Bill is excited to talk to Steve and listen to his stories and philosophies. It was indeed enlightening, but now to bid goodbye to a true friend would be very painful.

Bill is going to miss those morning breakfast, all that quality time he has been spending with Steve in the library, their talks, sharing the sweet old memories of their childhood, those coruscating stories and enlightening philosophies. The scintillating conversation with Steve, the erudition and the words of Steve, the brevity in his expression marked by simplicity, clarity and candor, which were like an avalanche of light, fulfilling Bill's heart and healing his wounds, would be an unforgettable memory.

Bill was immensely filled with elation with the overwhelming support and mental boost from Steve, the true and selfless companionship, and his compassionate guidance. Bill savored every moment with Steve.

Steve was a great solace during his debilitating period. Now being deprived of Steve's company, it would not be easy for Bill.

Steve is once again with Bill at the breakfast table. They have their breakfast and they move to the library.

Steve asks, "So Bill, how are you. I hope you are feeling good."

Bill says, "Yes Steve, feeling much better, except for the fact that you will be leaving today."

Steve smiles and says, "Don't worry Bill, I am not going to leave you alone, I have few good friends who will accompany you."

Bill asks surprisingly, "Friends, which friends?"

Steve replies, "Bill, my good friends are in your library. These books are my best friends. I am going to put you in the company of these eclectic books.

Bill, you have such a marvelous collection of books. It is just like a person already sitting on a treasure island and wondering to go for a voyage to find wealth.

Bill, start reading books. I have already selected some good books for you and placed them separately on the corner table. These books will enlighten you. Read them sincerely."

Bill says, "Thanks Steve, I appreciate your concern."

Steve and Bill are once again having their coffee and homemade Belgian biscuits.

Steve now asks, "So Bill, your question was how to come out of attachments of your family, your wife, your children. Probably you can get free from the bonds of your desires or the materialistic world, but how to get rid of these personal and emotional attachments. Is there a way?"

Bill says, "Yes Steve, please enlighten me in this regard."

Steve says, "Bill till the time you don't realize that everything in this world is just an image of the One, you won't be able to get out of these attachments. What we see as our family, our friends, our relatives all this is just an image of the One and only One. If we realize this fact, all attachments will go away in a trice."

Bill says, "I am sorry Steve, but I don't understand anything what you are saying. I cannot comprehend all this."

Steve says, "OK Bill. I will share one story with you.

This story, I heard from Swami Sarvapriyananda. He is a Hindu Monk and head of the Vedanta Society of New York. Vedanta is one of the world's most ancient religious philosophies and one of its broadest. Based on the Vedas, the sacred scriptures of India, Vedanta affirms the oneness of existence, the divinity of the soul, and the harmony of religions.

This is one of the most enlightening stories of Swamiji.

Once, there was a king. In his kingdom, a play was staged. In that play, there was a role of a little princess of Kashi. Kashi is an ancient city of India now known as Varanasi (Banaras). Unfortunately, they could not find anyone to play that role. However, the king discussed the problem with the Queen and she suggested that they can dress up their son as the princess, who was five years of age, and he will play the role of the princess. It was a good suggestion and everyone agreed.

On the very day, the prince was dressed up like a princess. When he got ready, he looked very beautiful. The Queen got enchanted by the looks of her son. She ordered, to make a good painting of her son, who was then looking as a beautiful princess. The order was followed quickly and the artist made the painting, capturing every little nuance of the princess's beauty. The painting looked resplendent, which could captivate anyone's attention.

Below the painting the artist wrote, "The princess of Kashi" and he mentioned the date on which the painting was made. The painting was finally preserved in a special room, in an ornate frame, behind a veil.

Time passed and after 15 years the prince grew young. Almost 20 years of age he started exploring the whole palace and all its room. One day he sees the old store in the palace and comes across this painting hidden behind a veil. As he removes the veil, he sees the painting of the beautiful princess of Kashi. The glory of her beauty, like an effulgence, touches the prince's heart. He sees the date and imagines that the princess is almost of his age. The prince beguiled by the beauty of the princess, falls in love with her. He wants to meet her but does not have any clue, where she lives. Moreover, the prince being shy in nature, could not share his feelings with anyone in the palace.

Day by day, his love is getting more intense, but there is no trace of finding the princess. The prince gets isolated and seems to be drenched in his emotions. He becomes vapidly listless and depressed. He feels as if his life is incomplete and worthless without the princess.

The prince remains in a lugubrious mood all the time, totally withdrawn, hardly speaking to anyone. Seeing this change in the prince's behavior, the king and the queen become gravely concerned. On the instructions of the king, one of his sagacious ministers, who is candor and wise, approaches the prince and asks him the reason for his plight.

He takes the prince into confidence and tells him, "You can confide in me and share your problem and I will try my level best to help you and resolve it."

The prince, having faith in the minister, confides. He says, "I am in love with a princess."

The minister says, "Oh vow, you are in love with a princess. Great!! Tell me her name and address. Give me her details and we can discuss for your marriage with her parents?"

The prince replies, "The problem is I never met her. I have just seen her painting, but the provenance of the painting is unknown. I have fallen in love with her. I want to meet her, but I have no clue of her address or where she resides."

The minister says, "Don't worry, show me her painting. I will try to get her details."

The prince now takes the minister to the room where the painting is kept. He takes out the veil and shows the painting of the princess to the minister.

The minister who has been working since long with the king, peruses the painting and recalls the complete matter. He looks at the prince, smiles and asks him to sit and listen.

He then reveals to the prince the entire incident, "Fifteen years ago a play was staged in the court and a little girl was required to play the role of a princess. Unfortunately, we could not find a girl to play that role. Hence your mother decided to dress you up like a princess. When you were dressed up, she was enchanted to see you, as you looked very beautiful and cute. She immediately ordered to make your painting. This painting that you see is not the princess of Kashi, but it is actually you. It is you, who is dressed up like a princess."

On hearing all this, the prince smiled in reminiscent. The moment he realized that the princess was none other than him, all his emotions disappeared. All the love and attachment in which he was so deeply drenched, vanished within seconds.

The story ends here."

Steve says, "Bill as long as there is duality, there will be attachments. But the moment we become one with the divine, all duality ceases, and all the attachments break within a second.

Hence when we contemplate on the One, the distance between us and that Supreme lessens and one day we merge with him. At this stage of realization, all attachments, bonding and affection will obliterate and finally just like the prince, we get rid of our emotional attachments.

I hope now the matter is clear, Bill."

"Fantastic Steve. Very clear and a didactic story," says Bill. "Steve I really wished I had listened to you much earlier. I was so obsessed with my desires that I had no time to listen to the ultimate truth of life. I understand I was like Charlie. I regret being so late."

Bill continues, "Fine Steve!! I want to give you something. Unfortunately, except money I have nothing. However, I can give you any amount of money you desire, just say once, it will be yours. I can give you so much, that your seven generations can stay financially free."

Steve smiles and says, "Bill you know money is insignificant to me."

Bill again insists, "Give me the figure Steve. If not for you then probably for something else. For some noble cause. I remember you wanted to make a church in our village. I would be pleased to auspice all the finance for it."

Steve replies, "Yes Bill, I wanted to build a church in our village long back, but now I have already constructed the church."

Bill asks surprisingly, "Where? In our village!!!, I didn't see any Church, I was recently there."

Steve replies, "Bill basically I wanted to do something meaningful in my life, though I had no inkling about what would be the most meaningful thing. Most of the good or holy things what we do, they just palliate and satisfy us momentarily, but after some time they lose their charm and once again we feel the emptiness within us. We are back to square one. However, as I understood life on a broader prospect, I realized, something meaningful means, that which would fulfill me and elevate me, irrevocably. Something which is not ephemeral. Not that would ostensibly look holy or sacred to the world, but that which makes me holy and sacred from within myself. Hence, I realized that it was immaterial to construct the church in the outside world. Often such acts enhance your vanity, rather than bringing fulfilment. So, I constructed the church within me. My mind has become the church, Bill.

God is now dwelling inside me; the church is within me. It is immaterial to make hundreds of churches, temples or mosques everywhere and proclaim yourself as a saintly person, if you cannot transform your own mind, to a place, where God can dwell.

Bill, the holiest place in the world should be within you. If a human being has not succeeded in his pursuit to sanctify his own mind, all his worldly goals and efforts are futile.

Bill, I enjoy and cherish all that is within me, with every breath I take, I feel God, the exuberance and the ineffable joy lies within me, nothing of the outside world, now entices me. I need nothing more. I feel fulfilled."

Bill is speechless. He understands, Steve has elevated to a different level. Bill becomes silent.

Steve says, "Fine Bill. Now I shall give you a small physical therapy and you shall be free from all the diseases in your body and shall be eased from all your ruminations. I shall just go outside to your garden to rejuvenate myself. I shall be back within ten minutes. After that when I ask you to close your eyes, just close them for few minutes. I shall put my fingers on your forehead for few seconds and all your tumor will go away gradually. So, Bill you sit here in the library, I shall be back within ten minutes."

Bill is unable to comprehend all this. However, Steve leaves to energize himself in the garden. After ten minutes, Steve is back in the library. He asks Bill to relax and close his eyes. Bill closes his eyes. He feels quite relaxed. After half a minute Bill feels Steve's fingers on his forehead. The touch is very gentle. Bill feels some energy, some divine power penetrating into his head, and then he feels the positive energy in his whole body. The fingers are removed. This touch was only for a few seconds, but Bill felt like he has some supernatural experience. After few minutes Steve asks Bill to open his eyes.

Bill says, "Divine!! Steve. It was a supernatural experience. I can't tell you. It is beyond my words to express."

Steve now speaks with absolute certitude, "Good Bill. Now you are perfectly fine. You have a perfect body and mind, there is no disease in your body. Your body has already started removing all unwanted things. Within few days you will feel younger, more energetic, you will be healthy as a new born child."

Bill is amazed and says, "Steve I have no words to express my gratitude to you. I want to speak but whatever I say would be so less and incomplete, it will not convey my feelings adequately. I am overwhelmed for everything that you have done for me. Steve, I thank you for everything. Thanks a lot."

Bill thanked Steve unceasingly with extreme deference.

Steve feels Bill's eternal gratitude for him. However, it is time for Steve to leave. Both of them shake hands and Steve departs.

CONCLUSION

AFTER ONE YEAR.

Steve is sitting in his garden. Suddenly a car arrives.

The driver opens the door and a very energetic man comes out from the car. This man looking sprightly, walks firmly, face transfigured with joy and happiness. He is Bill.

Bill looking young, agile, energetic and once again back with all his zeal, arrives there in front of Steve.

Steve feels very happy to see Bill and asks, "How are you, Bill?"

Bill says in a softened tone, "I am reborn Steve. All my ailments have gone forever. The miracle happened."

Bill further continues, "Steve I came to thank you. It is because of you that I am alive today. Not only alive, but I am so healthy, so energetic, I feel so joyful. My life which was full of despair, has turned to a life of boundless happiness. Through your intercession, I bestirred myself or else I was utterly bereft in my life. You are like a God to me. You are a living saint. You are divine Steve."

Steve smiles and says, "Bill, I did nothing."

Bill also smiles and replies, "Steve you are very generous and humble."

Steve says, "Bill, I can understand your feelings. But believe me I did nothing for you."

Bill speaks in surprising tone, "Steve, it is you who gave me the physical therapy. It is your hands which were on my forehead, which I felt. After that everything changed. Immediately after that moment, my tumor started healing, my pain vanquished and I started feeling better. All my energy came back, today I feel like a young boy. I have experienced the miracle in the energy of your hands."

Steve once again smiles and says, "Bill I know, but believe me, I did nothing."

Bill surprisingly asks, "Steve!! Why do you say like that? It is you, who vouchsafed. I would be happy if you would acknowledge this fact."

Steve smiles and says, "Bill I would happily concede to what you are saying, but the truth is something different. Things did not happen as it appears to you. Let me disclose the fact. Those fingers on your forehead were not mine. It was John, your driver. The fingers on your forehead, were John's fingers. I never laid my hands on your forehead, Bill."

Bill is totally awestruck and says, "What Steve, John!!!

My driver!!!

Are you serious!!!

Are you aware, what you are talking!!!"

Steve says, "Yes Bill. It was John. If you remember I went to your garden for ten minutes."

Bill says, "Yes I remember."

Steve says, "Infact I didn't go to your garden, I went to John. I asked John to help me and he agreed in good faith. I told him that all this has to be done secretly. So, when I came back to the library, I asked you to close your eyes. After that I beckoned John and he came silently. On my indication he put his hands on your forehead for a few seconds and then he left quietly. If you don't believe me, you can ask John."

Bill says, "I believe you Steve. I don't deny to what you are saying. But then how did I recover? I had that malignant tumor in my brain. Only after that experience, everything changed. Whatever happened, has happened under your auspices. Even my doctors were surprised. The miracle has still happened. I was supposed to die but I am still alive. All my medical reports are the evidence."

Steve says, "Bill, I know you had a malignant tumor and all that is true. I also know after that experience your condition started improving and your tumor disappeared like a miracle."

Bill asks, "So Steve, how did this happen?"

Steve replies, "OK Bill. Listen to me carefully now. I will tell you how this miracle happened.

You know Bill, I told you about Creation. If you remember I told you about the source. Bill this miracle has happened because of you. Bill the source is within you. I told you that all the supreme intelligence, all the divine energy, all the healing powers, everything is within you. It is you who has cured your own self. Neither me nor John, none of us has any role in this Bill. It is your will, your indomitable spirit, your connection with the supreme power, which has made it happened. It is all because of you Bill.

Bill, listen to me carefully. Nothing happens within you, without your permission and instructions. Everything within you happens, solely because of you. In the outside world things may happen without your permission, but within you, the whole area is under your authority. Once you take the control, everything comes and work under your command. So, Bill, whatever happened within you, it is solely because of you. You took the command, it is you who authorized this change and finally the whole universe conspired to work for you.

It was your indefatigable spirit that helped to cure your tumor. Bill, you have done it, you have achieved the impossible. Believe me, it is neither me nor John. I just showed you the direction. But it is you, who walked the path and came out from the imbroglios of difficulties.

Bill, as I said, don't underestimate yourself, you are a great person. You have that vehemence and fire within you. You fight with fortitude and tenacity; you have the unflinching grit and determination within you Bill. Bill it is your achievement.

Congratulations Bill. Congratulations!!!"

Once again Bill's eyes are moist with tears. Bill wants to profoundly thank Steve, but he is speechless.

However, Bill once again becomes pensive, but his eyes and heart are overflowing with gratitude for Steve. He is out of words but radiating sincere thanks to Steve.

After some time Bill asks Steve, "So now what Steve?"

Steve says, "Nothing Bill. Now we will have some Columbian coffee and I have some homemade Belgian biscuits. We will once again enjoy."

There is a serene smile on Bill's face and he says, "Good Steve."

While having the coffee Bill says, "Steve you seem to be quite rich. Your house is spacious and commodious, the furnishing and your garden, everything is quite elegant."

Steve replies, "Bill I never did anything to augment my income or contrived to gain anything for myself. Money just followed my skills."

Bill says, "Very nice Steve. I am very happy to see this."

As Bill and Steve are about to finish their coffee, Bill asks, "So what shall we do now Steve?"

Steve replies, "Bill ask John to go back and now you will stay here with me for a couple of days. We will go to our village and spend few days. We will once again enjoy the large expanses of green fields, the lovely sunshine, the beautiful woods, the earthy smell, the clear sky where you can count stars and the soft gentle zephyr. We will be far from the hustle and bustle of the city life, with the beauty of the nature, with the trees, flowers, mountains, streams, those sylvan solitudes, farmlands, cattle etc. We will see all the miracles of the nature, together in a salubrious environment. We will meditate joyously Bill. We will meditate."

There is a beatific smile on Bill's face and a perennial peace in his heart.

When life manifests, we cry,

When life grows, we try,

When life matures, the wisdom is introduced,

A new phase, with a new meaning is produced,

When life fails, we realize,

The fragility of our identities and importance of the divine,

When life ends, there is no noise,

The body vanishes, and the mind has no poise,

Let there be bliss, let the soul shine,

Let the body and spirit, merge into the divine.

www.ingramcontent.com/pod-product-compliance
Lightning Source LLC
LaVergne TN
LVHW050543160826
845677LV00011B/2163

* 9 7 9 8 8 8 9 8 6 9 3 7 5 *